# EVENINGS IN
## *Pasagarda*

### BRUNO CARLOS SANTOS
#### WITH ALAN SEEGER

559 PUBLISHING

Five59.com

Five59 Publishing

PO Box 212

Mission, SD 57555

www.Five59.com

First edition December 2015

FIVE59 and design are trademarks of Five59 Publishing, the publisher of this work.

For information about special discounts for bulk purchases, please contact Five59 Publishing at Five59.Publishing@gmail.com.

Interior and cover design by Five59 Publishing

Jacket illustration from a Creative Commons-licensed artwork obtained through splitshire.com.

Paperback edition:

ISBN-13: 978-1522743873
ISBN-10: 1522743871

Kindle edition:

ASIN:

# PROLOGUE:

Philip McReynolds was frantically trying to find his way out of the Tumbling Dice Club in a drunken state that would have caused many men of his young age to pass out. His best friend Henry was left to deal with the security staff. "Hey, man — I think you'd better get going," he told Philip. Meanwhile, many others were still partying and dancing, unaware of the brawl that had nearly erupted only a few moments earlier.

A red-haired girl named Tessa came to Philip, looking nervous and talking to him loudly, trying to be heard over the strident beat of the dance music. She'd been the cause of the earlier disagreement; her boyfriend hadn't liked the way Philip had looked at her, nor she at him.

She tried to say something to him, leaning in to be heard, but it was too loud, the alcohol in his blood too much. She reached out and touched a place on Philip's face, and despite his being so drunk, it hurt. "A bruise," she said. "You didn't have to…"

Henry saw the tall fellow she'd come in with approaching from across the room. He didn't look happy. "Philip," he called, trying to sound a warning.

Philip didn't answer. He needed air. Fresh air. He stumbled toward the nearest door, seeking the dull reddish glow of the emergency exit sign. Pushing through the crowd of partiers, he finally made it outside. Soaked in sweat, he felt a shiver run across his skin and shrugged. The magical effect of the booze was fading faster than he'd expected.

Still, his head felt too heavy. It seemed as if it were ready to fall off his shoulders and go rolling down the street. Philip thought of hailing a cab, but there were none in sight. He walked to the nearest corner, searching for a taxi, but ended up walking in circles, staggering and talking to himself. His words meant nothing; they were a bundle of random curses, pleas for forgiveness and vows of everlasting love. His eyes were covered by a fog of drunkenness and tears. Suddenly the bruise on his face began to ache, and along with that, his ribs as well.

In the seedy neighborhood where Philip found himself, he was surrounded by bars and clubs, all filled with other young drunks drowning themselves, as well as their sorrows, in mugs, glasses and bottles of beer, wine, or scotch. At one joint that advertised itself as a Tiki bar, a few opted for hollowed out pineapples, available for a few extra bucks, from which they sipped fruit flavored rum concoctions through long, thin straws. None of them looked outside; none of them were able to see Philip in his pursuit for a cab, getting dangerously close to the street — not until it was too late. A small group, ready to take the party homeward, came spilling out of the Tiki bar just in time to see Philip stumble into the narrow street. One of them cried out, "Watch out!" as loudly as someone who is somewhat inebriated could be expected to call, but not as loud as the screech of tires squealing on asphalt as the cab driver tried to stop his vehicle. The sound shocked the rest of the drunken partiers sober. Immediately afterward there was a dull thump, like a trash bag being tossed into a dumpster.

Philip felt as if his body was being swept up by a whirlwind. One moment he saw the heavily clouded sky, darkened by the mantle of the night. Rain was falling like a deluge now. In the next moment all he saw was blackness. A sense of peace came over him, though his body was broken and a trickle of blood dripped from his mouth and grew thicker with every breath he took. Philip lay on the asphalt, gazing towards the sky. In his haze of confusion, he saw a dark-haired girl running towards him, crying. It was Amanda.

In the crowd, he saw a Pierrot, a sad clown, a traditional character from the *Commedia dell'Arte* theatre. Philip had always felt an affinity for the sad-eyed character, and had a small figurine of one on his desk at home, but what was he doing here? He wasn't a real person... at least not any more. The commedia players had gone the way of the dinosaurs well more than a century ago. Pierrot stood there in his white costume, his sad expression, and his grey, rain cloud colored eyes, staring at Philip as he lay in the street.

Amanda knelt by Philip's side and frantically began to touch his face and torso as if she was trying to heal him by her very touch. She spoke to him tearfully, whispering low, so low that none of the others gathering around could make out what was said. But Philip, for whom the words were intended, didn't understand much of what she said either; the darkness was now encompassing him. He felt the soft touch of Amanda's hand, and the tears dripping from her eyes onto his wretched face.

"I love you, Amanda... so much..." he murmured.

"Philip... I love you too... I love you!" Amanda's voice dissolved into sobbing. All she could do now was utter a single cry as a peaceful smile came to Philip's lips.

"What did he say?" muttered one of the people in the gathering crowd to the young woman who was kneeling over him.

"I'm not sure... I think he said 'I love you,' and he seems to think I'm someone named Amanda."

*April. I've just turned fifteen.*

*I will not say "Dear Diary," because this isn't really a diary... and besides, that sounds terribly old-fashioned. But for some reason, I want to make this a daily ritual. For some, this might be forcing them to be something they are not, but for me it isn't... I don't have anyone else to talk to, so this journal will be where I share my thoughts and hopes and dreams.*

*Today I had another fight with my mother. She simply does not understand me, and she doesn't make even the slightest effort to try. She yells at me, always saying that I am nothing but a dreamer... But I wonder sometimes (ALL the time, really!) what is so wrong with dreaming...? We all dream, isn't that right? People live for dreams. The world is powered by dreams.*

# 1: THE ECCENTRIC BOOKSELLER

The sky was covered with thick clouds, like huge smokescreens. The wind was blowing intensely, practically screaming. It was clear that a heavy rain was on its way. Since it was the season for it, many people in the street were carrying umbrellas. Still, there were a handful of individuals who were braving the weather conditions without such valuable protection, and those poor souls kept glancing towards the awnings of nearby buildings, ready to rush towards them for shelter at the first sign of raindrops hitting the ground.

A fuzzy-haired boy named Philip was watching them with a slightly sadistic amusement. He was a rather clumsy, extremely melancholy sort of individual; he was well known among his tiny circle of friends for having light eyes, not blue or green but the color of the rain. Still, watching people sometimes gave him the opportunity to put himself into a good mood.

*These people must think they're made out of paper, to be so afraid of the rain.* He thought of them as *les gens effrayés sans parapluie.*

But even more than the simple, cheap mockery of people passing by, the thing that made Philip truly happy was the rain itself. He had always loved the rain. Even more, he loved the smell of it and the feel of the heavy drops splattering on his skin.

He was walking alone down the sidewalk when he heard the unmistakable sound of distant thunder. Philip smiled broadly when he heard two loud claps of thunder and the first drops began to fall. By that time, many people on the streets had already begun to run for shelter.

Philip felt a cold raindrop strike the tip of his nose and then the rain began to fall in its full glory — powerful, noisy, and cleansing. There was something almost spiritual about it. Philip stood in the rain, allowing himself to be purified, and while some of his fellow pedestrians hurried to open their umbrellas, others — most of whom were already soaked to the skin — were rubbing their arms for warmth under the shelter of the nearest awning.

Philip made no effort to hurry out of the downpour or to rush his pace. Instead, he breathed in deeply in order to catch the distinct scent of the cold rain hitting the hot asphalt, allowing it to penetrate deeply into his lungs.

As everyone around stared at him with curiosity, Philip walked along the street with nimble steps. He was now less than two blocks away from his destination: an imposing-looking, recently remodeled building on Brazil Street.

It was a fortress-like structure guarded by gates and iron railings which had once been a tenement renowned for its rodent infestation, now completely renovated and really quite beautiful. The only possible communication with the doorman — who, on this stormy day, sat comfortably on his warm, dry perch inside — was to buzz him via the intercom. As Philip approached, the doorman's brow knitted in worry. His boss — a tall, skinny fellow who had the habit of twisting the ends of his thin, curved mustache between his index finger and thumb — had given him strict instructions to keep the elegant, red velvet carpet that covered the floor and the stairs of the lobby dry and clean by any means necessary, even on rainy days. In fact, *especially* on rainy days.

"How the hell am I supposed to keep the goddamn carpet dry in this mess?" wondered the doorman. "I suppose he expects me to suck it up with a straw."

By now, Philip was drenched head to toe, and the guardian of the lobby, as the doorman thought of himself, knew that once he was granted access to the lobby, the carpet would soon be soaked as well.

*Oh, please,* thought the doorman, *don't come any closer. Go somewhere else. Anywhere but here.* But despite his mental attempts to dissuade Philip's approach, the young man pressed the buzzer. Any hope of keeping the carpet flawlessly clean faded as the doorman replied:

"Good morning, sir... what can I do for you?"

"Good morning," replied Philip, choking slightly on the waterfall that cascaded from the top of his head to his lips. "I'd like to see Mr. Muñoz."

"Mr. Muñoz? Would that be Mr. Muñoz on the fifth floor?"

"Just a second," Philip said, rummaging through his pockets. He finally found a piece of paper that looked as if it had been trampled underfoot. It was shredded and the ink was smeared, but he could still make out the name and address:

*Mr. Alonso Fausto Hidalgo Muñoz*
*59 Brazil Blvd., 5th Floor*
*Re: E. Bovary*

"Yes," Philip said. "Mr. Alonso Fausto Hidalgo Muñoz. I'm supposed to pick something up from him."

"And your name, sir…?"

"Philip. I'm Philip."

"Hold on, Mr. Philip, I'm calling Mr. Muñoz."

The intercom rang twice in the Muñoz apartment, and then a voice answered with the same temper that had made him so famous in the neighborhood.

"By a thousand demons!" muttered the old Spaniard. "It's not enough that those damned drunkards have to hang around my shop — now it looks like they're coming to torment me at home as well… Well, what is it?" he asked the doorman.

"There's a guy down here — a *kid,* really — who says he's here to pick something up from you."

"What? No. Tell him I don't have anything for him."

"Okay, but…"

"But what?!"

"Well, he says he's here with a request from a Ms. Bovary?"

The name Bovary had a sudden, dramatic effect on Muñoz's mood. He told the doorman to send the young fellow up.

The doorman warned Philip to watch out for the red carpet as much as possible, even though he knew that there was very little that Philip could do to avoid it being soiled, and directed him to the elevator. Philip tiptoed across the lobby and pressed the button marked 5.

Upon reaching the corresponding floor, Philip found himself in a hallway — really no more than a dimly lit foyer the size of a standard hotel room — adorned with a corner table with elaborately carved feet, atop which a sat a large vase of artificial flowers. At the other end of the foyer was a single door made of blackened, highly polished wood. Philip thought it might be ebony.

There was only a single apartment per floor in this building, and this imposing door led to Fausto Muñoz's lair. Even by the standard of what Philip's father pulled in — and he did quite well for himself, having started his law firm shortly after finishing at CUNY Law and later branching out into real estate holdings — living in a rent-controlled building with only a couple of rooms on each floor was a luxury few could afford, let alone full floor units such as these.

Philip could recall his father saying, "It's kind of funny how often people who come to America from other countries seem to do better for themselves than people who were born here." He rang the exquisite looking bell at Muñoz's door. The sound was sharp and shrill, giving Philip the impression that someone was stabbing him in the ear with an icepick.

Muñoz must have felt the same, for from within the apartment came a fearsome battle cry as if he was fully unaware that a visitor was about to ring the bell.

*"¡Pinche idiota!* I'm *coming!"*

The dark, wooden door opened with a creak, revealing a man in his late 50s, standing five foot five or so, with such a hardened expression on his face that it seemed as if it were carved out of the same wood as the door. Philip choked back his fear at the man's apparent animosity and armed himself with the broad smile that he found so handy in these kinds of awkward situations.

"Good morning, sir. My name is Philip McReynolds. It's very nice to meet you, Mr. Muñoz...?"

Muñoz's face was impassive. "You've come here to get the book, right?"

"The book for Miss Bovary... Yes." Philip hesitated, then continued, "She told me — Miss Bovary did, I mean — that you were the owner of Muñoz Antiquities and Books, and, well... after Mr. Bovary died... uh... he was the owner of Bovary Antiques in Garden City... but I guess you know that already... I'm sorry. Anyway, I came here because of..."

"Café Crème, Volume I," Muñoz said with a wry smile that seemed to be a sadistic mockery, yet with a touch of sympathy.

"Y-yes..." Philip replied.

Muñoz then burst into a friendly laugh, and putting his arm around Philip's neck as if they were lifelong friends, pulled him into the apartment.

"Get on board, *ninõ* — no need to worry!"

Fausto Muñoz's apartment smelled of lavender and mahogany. As far as Philip could see, it was ornately decorated with the most exquisite furniture that money could buy. In the living room, behind a beautiful, mirror-black Steinway grand piano stood eight tall, broad shelves lined one wall, crammed with more books than one could count. Yet Muñoz quickly found the one particular book among them and held it out to Philip.

"Here you go, *niño!*"

Philip smiled, pulled his wallet from his left hip pocket, and began to count out some bills. Muñoz smiled back — a slightly frightening visage — and told him, "It's already taken care of. But would *you* like to do some business, *niño?*"

"Well, it depends on…"

Muñoz didn't let Philip finish his sentence. "What if I were to let you take another one along? Free of charge, of course."

"Another book? That would be great."

"I knew you would like it, *niño.* You got that bookish sort of look, and not without reason." He tapped his temple. "You're smart. I can tell."

"Well... thanks..." He wasn't sure if it was a compliment or not.

"Actually, I really like this book. But there's something about it... someone used it as their diary... a *girl*... and I'm afraid the story does not end very well."

Philip waited for him to go on.

"And to be honest," the older man continued, "I'm kind of tired of sad stories."

*So am I,* thought Philip.

Muñoz returned to his shelves and retrieved a book, then walked back to Philip. In his huge hands was an exceptionally old book with worn, hard fabric-covered covers, the pages stained brown with age.

"In the current state, this book would be worth almost nothing. On the other hand, if you consider the emotional value, It would be difficult to find anyone willing to offer the ridiculous amount it would be worth. I haven't the stomach to simply throw it away like so much *basura*... I feel bad, to imagine something so personal and intimate being crushed along with a mess of potato peels and empty tin cans."

"Okay," replied Philip. He noticed Muñoz's eyes becoming moist. He was amazed at how emotional this man, who had seemed so rough, could be.

"And you know, *niño*... the *niña* who used this book for her diary... looking at you, I think you two would have made a nice couple."

Philip said nothing, unsure of how he should respond.

"You have a girlfriend, *niño?*"

"No, Mr. Muñoz... I don't... not exactly. Not yet."

"Well, I think if somehow you could meet this girl, she'd have been a perfect match for you," said Muñoz, now smiling broadly. Then his expression darkened slightly. "If she were still with us, I mean."

Philip spent only a few more minutes in Muñoz's apartment, and then left, telling the doorman in the lobby goodbye as he left.

He saw that the heavens, while still heavy with clouds, were no longer pouring rain. He was pleased at this. He loved the rain, but he didn't want to risk the precious books being damaged.

Taking the long way home, he opened the plastic bag that Muñoz had given him and pulled out the mysterious gift book. The pages were yellowed like the leaves of autumn trees, and Philip glanced at a few pages from "The Diary of Kasumi."

He saw that the book was heavily annotated, with notes and underlines and many circled words. Inside the front cover was a name: *Kasumi.* There were Japanese Kanji characters below it, as well, perhaps repeating what was written in English? He wasn't sure. About two-thirds of what was written was in Japanese.

The writing was so delicate that it was hard to believe it was written by human hands. Philip ran his eyes over each line. It seemed to be the diary of a teenage girl, who constantly complained about her mother and about something else that Philip knew only too well: loneliness. He closed the book and headed home, thinking that it wouldn't have been a bad thing to meet this girl, but Muñoz had indicated that she was… what? Dead? It saddened Philip to think so.

*April. I've just turned fifteen.*

*I will not say "Dear Diary," because this isn't really a diary... and besides, that sounds terribly old-fashioned. But for some reason, I want to make this a daily ritual. For some, this might be forcing them to be something they are not, but for me it isn't... I don't have anyone else to talk to, so this journal will be where I share my thoughts and hopes and dreams.*

*Today I had another fight with my mother. She simply does not understand me, and she doesn't make even the slightest effort to try. She yells at me, always saying that I am nothing but a dreamer... But I wonder sometimes (ALL the time, really!) what is so wrong with dreaming...? We all dream, isn't that right? People live for dreams. The world is powered by dreams.*

*I think everyone dreams... except for her. My mother has always been so bitter and surly. I think that she was born old...*

*From a very sad and lonely Kasumi.*

# 2: THE SHADOW OF JULIA

Philip rolled in his bed, burrowing into his covers, burying his head beneath the pillow like a worm trying desperately to return to the moist soil on a summer's day. Three weeks had passed since he had met the eccentric Mr. Fausto Muñoz, and since then, the Diary of Kasumi had become his constant companion. The book lay on his nightstand, near his head, where he had laid it in the wee hours of the night when he discovered he could no longer keep his eyes open enough to read it.

Though it felt like he had only shut off the light moments before to go to sleep, his alarm clock continued to ring, emitting a sharp, deafening sound like a hail of bullets hitting a cathedral bell.

Apart from hiding his head under the pillow, however, Philip seemed to completely ignore the fact that it was time to get up, and made one last desperate attempt to silence the beast, trying to smother the thing with his pillow. It was futile, however. By the time he was cognizant of the alarm, Philip was fully awake. He rubbed his eyes with both hands until they were red below the eyelids.

With all the vigor of a turtle, Philip sat up on the side of his narrow, wooden bed, shutting off the alarm by slamming his hand down on the button with much more force than was necessary. Philip ran his fingers through his hair gently, with his eyes closed, and for a moment he imagined that a woman's hand was caressing him. For a few seconds, he drifted off into imagination… then he shook his head, opened his eyes, and saw his true surroundings. He was alone in a small room, beige paint peeling off the walls. A couple of small, mismatched bookshelves and a desk and chair were the only furniture other than his bed. Cardboard boxes of books dotted most of the floor.

It was 6:00 AM. Philip always had the habit of setting the "banshee," as he referred to the alarm clock, to wake him at that time. He wanted — no, he *needed* plenty of time to prepare for the day, since he had never been able get ready as quickly as other people. He was, as many said, a "miserably slow person."

He lived with his mother, Julia, in a run-down apartment which was cluttered with antique furniture and paintings which had never been hung on the walls, and stacks of boxes, many of which seemed never to have been opened. Crammed with painful memories and dusty objects, that old apartment was the physical manifestation of Philip's emotional fuzziness.It was the very antithesis of the elegance of Muñoz's place.

The floor of the apartment was covered with mahogany parquets in various shades of brown. Much of the antique furniture was covered with sheets. The only neatly arranged thing in the entire place was a wide-ranging collection of books, mostly art and classic works bought by Julia herself for reference, as well as some works on law and economics that had been brought from her estranged husband Anthony's office. Philip had his own small collection of books that he had gathered, including a poetic anthology by a Brazilian author named Manuel Bandeira.

Julia had always been delicate and extremely emotional, much like Philip. In her youth, she had tried to pursue a painting career, but could never rise above the status of gifted amateur. It was a source of deep frustration and led her to embrace the lifestyle and role of a housewife with great enthusiasm as a balm to ease the pain of her fruitless artistic career.

Still, over the years, Julia sought to convince herself and everyone around her that she had given up her career to devote herself to her son and her husband. In fact, Julia had succeeded in convincing even herself. "For you and your father, I gave up everything," Julia would say to little Philip.

It felt safe, but proved a mistake. Having grown to see her marriage as the only reason for her existence, she plunged into a state of severe depression when Anthony left her, deciding that Julia's instability was an undesirable factor in his life. These days, Julia spent most of her free time in her room, under heavy medication.

Philip often passed in front of his mother's door, which seemed as if it were hermetically sealed. His toes twitched as if they were trying to grab at the mahogany floor, marking a constant, silent vigil. Holding his breath, Philip slowly approached his mother's bedroom door. A sense of deep sadness seemed to linger there, as if emanating from Julia and penetrating the eroded wood. Inside the room, other than the oppressive feeling, there was only the sound of a serene and rhythmic breathing that emerged from what was otherwise absolute silence.

Although it seemed sealed, Julia's door was never locked. Perhaps she feared that she might misjudge her medications at some point. Philip turned the knob and pushed the door open carefully, quietly. Julia's room was the one place in the dwelling that, although seeming completely unkempt and neglected, gave off an air of nobility as if the room had settled into its misery, still not yet fully accepting it, and even more unwilling to assimilate it.

There was a picture which had been painted by the young Julia many years before, one of dozens, none of which she had ever sold, decorating one of the walls: A *Pierrot,* a sad clown, lying helpless, being stalked by a sphinx. There were other strange things going on in the painting as well. Philip had never paid too much attention to it, finding it too strange to comprehend. A pair of satin curtains filtered the sunlight that occasionally dared to pass through the window. A nightstand of noble proportions stood below the painting, next to the beautifully crafted bed.

On the king size bed, covered with (slightly yellowed) white sheets lay a light-skinned woman wearing a silk robe. This was Julia. Her robe was tied so loosely that one of her full breasts was half exposed. Her face, still pretty, was partly concealed by her long hair, hanging in thick curls in three or four different shades of brown, from nearly black to almost blonde, Julia's strategy to disguise the increasing number of grey strands.

Philip approached and caressed her face, as she used to do for him years before when he was a small child, and even later on, when he was no longer a boy. He proceeded to touch her carotid, feeling for the slow and steady pulse. Still, she didn't move a muscle apart from those necessary for her breathing. Philip felt relieved and left the room. He felt that Julia would always be there, resting peacefully.

After descending two flights of stairs, Philip spent a few seconds in the lobby of the building, checking the mailbox. Due the frequent rain in recent weeks, there was a problem of seepage in the ceiling and it had begun to burst, literally. Philip tried to dodge the drips while opening the mailbox. There were no letters, messages or anything else personal, only pizza circulars and an endless number of bills.

The building itself was small, only four floors, and had been built a few years after World War II. It had no elevator, doorman, or even a janitor. Although the absence of these amenities, which were so common in other modern buildings, represented some discomfort, it also meant that it was less expensive to live there, which was something that made it very attractive.

The owners of the building — some said it was an organized crime family, others a Jewish syndicate — whether for lack of resources or lack of interest, seldom performed maintenance. Except when pipes would burst or walls crumble, which had occurred more than once, the only thing of their concern was the color of the façade, which had been changed from a light shade of blue to yellow less than two months ago; now it had been repainted a salmon color just this week. Who knew how long it would it take for the color to be changed yet again?

# 3: THE SPHINX

One day Philip was browsing through some of his mother's books of art and came across an image that fascinated him. It was the figure of a woman, who had a beautiful face of granite with zirconium eyes. Her nude torso proudly displayed pear-shaped breasts. Her human form ended at the hips, and became the body of a lion. Instead of hands, she had the legs of a lion as well, with great black claws on the paws. Her tail was a snake, and from her shoulders stretched great wings like those of an eagle.

From that day forward he was fascinated by the idea of such a creature, and wondered what it was that had inspired the artist to create it.

# 4: PIERROT

There was a *Pierrot* — a sad clown — whose skin was the color of lead and whose eyes were the color of the rain. He was dressed in fabrics made from sad memories and vain hopes, adorned with gray hours and the tears of patient waiting. He wandered the shadows, crying for the days that never came and lives that were never lived.

Pierrot was not so much buffeted by the pain from the injuries he had never suffered as he was dominated by fear.

Waiting... Pierrot understood that his cries came only to the ears of Kairos. καιρός is a Greek word meaning the opportune moment for something to happen. Waiting for the right time, for Pierrot, meant he would find the time and place where he would no longer be alone.

However, to get to this place, Pierrot had to submit to being trussed up with a large rope called "Patience." Thus, the gray figure was driven by hopes that he would finally arrive at the place he called Pasargada.

This is what he had hoped for; however, it was a lie: Pierrot was not led to Pasargada. Instead, he was locked in a tall tower called the Kairos Tower, where he was not permitted to leave. His only contact with the outside world was a small window where he could see the city of Pasargada. Pierrot was sentenced, along with many other figures who were deceived by their expectations and confined there.

Inside the tower was a large library, taken by the dust of time, where vast volumes were written in blood and tears on autumn leaves and seeds that died before being germinated. In the armory were countless broken swords, dented coats of armor and shattered shields, all covered with moss and green lichens and dissolving into red rust.

In the lower parts of the tower, there was a man who called himself the king, once having pulled a sword from a stone, who lived in dreams and memories of a time of greatness. Once his beard and his long hair had been golden, but they were now the scraggly grey of an old man.

Next to the room where the king resided was a chamber filled with women without faces, whose bodies seemed to have been carved in Aphrodite's image by the hands of Eros, shapely enough to please Bacchus.

On the floor above the king lived a knight who had witnessed the winter's first snowfall so many times that he had lost count. He had traveled the world, sword in hand, but had been beaten down by wooden giants. He sat in his room, crying over sad memories, and for his lost love who had perished many springs before.

Pierrot shared his dungeon with Banshee as well, who constantly harangued the others, making their ears bleed.

Day after day through the frosted glass, the gray eyes of Pierrot beheld Pasagarda.

Manuel Bandeira wrote of Pasagarda half a century ago, in a poem. He was a Portuguese poet and literary critic.

Pasagarda was the name of the capitol city built by King Cyrus of Persia in the 6th century BCE. It was also the location of his tomb. When Bandeira wrote, "I'm going to Pasagarda," in a way, he was saying both that he was going to the place he considered his paradise and his ultimate resting place, and that he was going to a place where he would have everything that he had ever wanted.

Pierrot had found Pasagarda, but it was on the other side of a great stone wall, the walls of his prison.

The people of that city were happy, always smiling, laughing and conversing. They hummed and danced the Viennese waltz, eating and drinking. Their clothes were made of sunlight, autumn afternoons and spring mornings, and they were adorned with pieces of stars and fragments of the Moon. The smiles on their faces were perennial and their days were filled with constant laughter. Their eyes were like the sky over the clouds, as lakes inside the most beautiful woods, like the dawn and sunset. And because they were so happy, sitting at a banquet table, while Pierrot sat in his dank, dark cell, he envied them.

Pierrot wanted the sun, but its rays scorched his pale skin and blinded his rain-colored eyes. There was no remedy. Pierrot was to remain there, guarded by impassable walls, with the only means of contacting Pasargada being the glimpse that he had through the tiny window. The sun shone cold through that small portal, its rays like tentacles of infinite length, which could be molded into any shape or size, being able to penetrate through small cracks and slowly fill rooms of grand dimensions. It illuminated a world where Pierrot would never be welcome. For pierrot, there was only the gray silence.

The time flowed. Pierrot did not know if it was years, decades, centuries or even millennia. There was no longer any feeling or emotion. Everything had become white and opaque. There was no ivory or ebony, but only ashes. Even the white had yellowed further, and the embroideries were corroded. Tears the color of burnished silver flowed from Pierrot's eyes continuously from dawn to sunset. Perhaps his eyes were crumbling, dissolved by so many tears.

One day, however, through the frosted glass window, the nearly blind Pierrot realized that one of the people of the city was looking at him. He wore a full moon, and on his left arm, cradled a snake the color of desert sand. He seemed to be trying to say something to Pierrot, but even if he had shrieked like the Banshee, from this distance, the cry would be less than the whisper of a lover in the ears of his beloved. However, the man was insistent and through much effort, made himself understood. He gave his name and explained that he was writing a *maqama,* which literally means "assemblies." originally an Arabic literary form combining rhymed prose with intervals of poetry.

His maqama, however, needed a living character, so he asked Pierrot, the gray clown, to be the main character of his writing.

Pierrot said he knew nothing of how to do this, explaining that he was a little deaf and almost blind, feeling cold and afraid, expecting, with the loss of his vision, to soon be completely engulfed in darkness. The man agreed to help him if he would agree to be the protagonist of his maqama. Although he had no inkling of what this was, he agreed.

The man then taught him a means of escape from the dungeon; it was a very simple incantation. Pierrot was to approach the window and place his lips against it; in doing so, he would allow himself to believe, as never before, that it was possible to bring down the massive walls of the tower and reach Pasargada.

As he did so, a damsel extended her hands, touching those of Pierrot as if there was no window or wall between them. She had the voice of a nymph and her skin was covered with perfume: Italian mandarin, orange blossoms, and peaches, pink star jasmine, peony, rosewood and amber. To touch her, Pierrot had to close his eyes, and she would lead him gently through the walls and the window, as if both were made of fog.

There were, however, conditions, and if, even for a brief moment, Pierrot violated any of them, she would abandon him and leave, never to return. Pierrot would be in prison again, the walls become solid, and would remain there, in the very passage where he had been abandoned. Whether it was with half of his body inside the prison, or with only his head in Pasargadae. The woman would not shed a tear, even if Pierrot was slowly baked by the sun until he was blind and was finally reduced to ashes.

Upon hearing this, Pierrot was afraid, but still approached the window and touched it with his lips. After a split second that seemed to last for an eternity, the icy touch of glass and ivory was replaced by the warm and soft touch of the girl's lips. Pierrot smelled the delicate scent of jasmine and the soft arms of Colombina enveloped him. She whispered in his ears to open his eyes. Everything was light. Pierrot had never seen anything as beautiful and delicate as his Colombina. She was more beautiful than Aphrodite; her smile overshadowed the sun itself. Her hair was long, the color of mahogany, and wavy as the high tides. Her eyes were a mixture of sardonyx and amber. Her body was covered with blue cloth, the color of the sky, midnight and dusk, adorned with gold and silver lights. At that moment, the lips of every one of the countless people of Pasagarda flowed with one sacred melody, like the songs of the Renaissance as if they were a choir conducted by his own Colombina, whose voice would make Dione herself blush.

Pierrot then recited the rules that could never be broken: "Do not touch Colombina if she has not asked for your touch. Do not seek Colombina's lips if she has not asked for your kisses. Do not ask for her, even though your heart is shattered with longing. Accept the momentary wait, for it is not eternal. Do not smother the fire, or there will be only cold. Do not overwhelm the Nymph, or she will become a Sphinx. Simply love. Love what is to be loved; love her for who she is.

"I can see...!" said Pierrot, his eyes full of tears, no longer blinded. "I can *see!*"

"Yes," answered Colombina with her melodious voice. "Your eyes are no longer clouds and rain, but the sky above them. Everything is light."

"The way you touched my face... ran your fingers through my hair..." His eyes lit up, filled with a sweetness that he never knew could exist.

Then Colombina told him that she loved him, and would never leave him; and so began the maqama...

# 5: ANTHONY

Growing up in Brooklyn, New York, Anthony McReynolds's best friend was a shrewd little con man named Frankie Andretti. From the time he and "Tony" were in the sixth grade — around twelve years old — Frankie was a smooth-talking, quick-witted wheeler and dealer who was able to manipulate practically anyone they met into doing whatever he wanted them to, from giving him things like records and tapes or jewelry to, later on, letting him borrow their cars or talking girls into going out with him.

When they graduated from high school, Frankie had big plans to go on to college and then on to law school, after which he planned to make a mint as a high dollar attorney in Manhattan.

There were rumors about Frankie's family — that they had mob connections, or even that his father, Bernardo, was a *soldato* (soldier) for one of the several organized crime families in the area, or at the very least an associate. Ostensibly, he was a butcher, but as often as not, he was curiously absent from the shop when people stopped in to ask for the choice cuts of meat that he was famous for.

The summer after Frankie graduated, Bernardo died unexpectedly, and the truth came out. Bernardo had been a kidney patient for nearly eleven years. He was absent from the butcher shop so often because he was undergoing dialysis three times a week; he had never allowed anyone in his family to reveal his health condition to anyone else.

His death left his family nearly penniless. Because his family didn't have the money for his college tuition, Frankie decided to sign up for a four-year hitch in the United States Marines under a program where they would pay for him to go to school following his time in the Corps.

In April of 1980, Frankie's unit was selected as part of the combined task force for Operation Eagle Claw, the mission ordered by President Jimmy Carter to attempt the rescue of 52 diplomats that were being held captive at the U.S. Embassy in Tehran, Iran.

Among other problems, one of the helicopters crashed into a EC-130 transport plane containing both servicemen and jet fuel. The resulting fire destroyed both aircraft and killed eight servicemen, including Frankie.

In his best friend's honor, Anthony changed his major from Accounting to Political Science with a pre-law emphasis, deciding that he would go on to law school and fulfill Frankie's dream. He graduated from The College of New Jersey with his Bachelor's in 1983 and went on to law school at City University of New York, graduating in 1986.

Following his graduation ceremony, he and a half-dozen or so friends went out to celebrate. They went to their favorite watering hole, Rudy's on 9th Avenue.

There, he met a girl; her name was Julia.

# 6: MADAME BOVARY

Henry Ratajczik, the vulgar and often profane "Ratso," was a tall boy with an easy smile, the smile of those who practice with impunity acts that would result in the condemnation of others. Philip and Henry met in grade school, when they were small. They had known each other at an even younger age, because their mothers were close friends, practically sisters, but they had never spent much time together apart from that.

However, their first meeting at school had involved an incident on the playground when they were just eleven. Henry and Philip were being bullied by a trio of older boys. In almost every similar situation, Henry the Rat came out on top, but on this day the balance of power was tilted in favor of the bullies. Despite that, Philip harbored no grudge against Henry. They had become fast friends.

Now both young men were nineteen. The two often met for coffee or pie from time to time, sometimes planned and other times at random when Philip was wandering through the park, generally on Sunday afternoons.

This particular occasion was one of the unplanned ones. Henry simply stumbled on Philip while he was walking down the street, carrying a bag containing the Diary of Kasumi.

When asked what was in the bag, Philip declined to reveal its contents. Henry suspected it contained a notebook in which Philip was writing poetry, or perhaps a novel. In any case, he could see that Philip was in a melancholy mood, of the sort that made Henry refer to him at times as 'Hamlet.'

Philip always welcomed such an opportunity to spend time with Henry, mostly because it meant not having to be at home with his mother. They spent hours discussing such frivolities as the gender of angels, whether black holes led to alternate universes, and whether Superman could pick up Mjolnir.

And so the two sat at the nearest Starbuck's on this cold and rainy afternoon. Philip always welcomed the opportunity to spend time away from his dismal apartment. Finally, the subject turned to the return of an old mutual friend.

"How old do you think a woman has to be before they'd call her Madame?" Henry asked Philip.

"I dunno... forty, maybe?"

"Oh, no, man! I'd say at least fifty..."

"Emma's not a Madame, then."

"Nope. But still, she's way out of *your* league, dude."

Philip didn't say a word, but his eyes betrayed him.

"Well," Henry said with a low chuckle. "You must have a thing for mature women."

Philip smiled, but was silent.

As Henry had grown up, he had crafted that easy smile into one that was specifically designed to attract girls. His tastes, views and temper made him the very antithesis of Philip, but still, due to the many years that they had known each other, Henry had always been Philip's best — and only — friend.

"Are you excited, Philip?"

"Well, actually..."

"Don't fuckin' lie to me, Phil — I'm your best friend, remember?"

Philip remained quiet, staring at the ground, his face red as a chili pepper, a sure sign that Henry was right.

"Ah, man, I always knew you had a crush on her..."

"Not really."

"Don't give me that bullshit! I ain't buyin' it, bitch!" laughed Henry. "Remember how everyone called her 'Auntie Em' except for you?"

"To tell you the truth, I remember very little from that time."

"Did anybody ever tell you that you fucking *suck* at lying?"

Philip fell silent again.

"She must be, what? Ten years older than us...?"

*"Six* years older," interrupted Philip.

Henry smiled. Philip looked up and realized he had given himself up.

According to Philip's calculations, Emmanuelle Bovary was 25 years old now. Despite still looking like she could be in her teens to the eyes of the two young men, Emma Bovary was a mature woman, and in every way, completely fascinating.

Emma was tall — some might even say excessively tall, at 5'10" — and slender. She had long, curly butterscotch hair. Her eyes were expressive, bright, almond-shaped and hazel-colored, and her face was perfectly symmetrical and delicate. She was always well dressed and wore Fleur de Cabotine.

Philip found her lips particularly attractive, especially when she spoke. They seemed to take on the form of a cherry. She had been born and spent the first decade of her life in Paris. Her French accent was endearing, and her ways were much more polite than one might expect. For someone so attractive, it would be not uncommon for her to be taken for an arrogant person. Philip didn't think she was arrogant... well, maybe just a little. But it wouldn't matter. Her perfume and her cool demeanor had been lodged in his memories for the past thirteen years or so.

They had first met when Emma was in her early teens. At that time, Anthony's law practice had not grown to what it was at present. He was living, along with Julia and Philip — who was then seven years old — in a small apartment in Brooklyn, so small that it prevented any sort of intimacy between the young couple, since their son shared the room.

"This kid is driving me crazy," Anthony often complained.

The only oasis amidst this desert reality was Benoit Bovary, an elderly Frenchman, wise and patient. He was only moderately successful at that point, but offered three things which Anthony welcomed: pleasant conversation, often in French; exciting games of chess, and, in particular, a nearly endless need for legal services, which Anthony was happy to provide.

Benoit appreciated Anthony, but found the American young and naïve, and often wished the lawyer would be a little more aggressive, though he completely understood his ways. Anthony had gone through a difficult time while finishing school, struggling for scholarships and buying used books.

*"Le monde n'est pas seulement milieu sauvage;* the world is not a jungle," Benoit would often say to his lawyer. It wouldn't work, at least not as well as he hoped. Despite nourishing both respect and gratitude for Monsieur Bovary, it was difficult to see how someone who had never experienced hardships could give advice to a soul as battered as Anthony. The world was, indeed, a jungle, and to survive, it was necessary to become a predator.

Philip's father, Anthony, considered Benoit a weak-hearted man. The Frenchman had one daughter, Emmanuelle, who lived half the year with her mother in California after a rather messy divorce. A few years later, Emma's mother passed away, and Benoit moved to Los Angeles to finish raising his daughter. She had not been particularly happy there, however. Unlike her father, who loved the heat of the Southern California sun, Emma did not like the tropical weather, the food or the way people around her behaved. She continually asked to move back to New York.

Emma's skin had never adapted to the blazing sun of Los Angeles; her stomach did not find the typical teenage diet of In-n-Out Burgers, food truck fare, and milk shakes agreeable, and she preferred the strains of Brahms and Mendelssohn to the music of the dance clubs, which reminded her of cat's claws scratching a blackboard.

Her complaints were plentiful and common: "Why does everyone wear sandals or athletic shoes? The infernal heat... Oh, *père,* my face is all full of sores!"

The only comfort Emma had was when the handsome lawyer visited them from New York to discuss business with her father. He was undoubtedly a vigorous man. Blue, piercing eyes, full of an innate aggressiveness and a posture that emanated power.

"How handsome..." sighed Emma every time she laid eyes on Anthony. He was like a Greek god in a suit.

Within few years, they moved back to New York, where Monsieur Bovary rebuilt his antique shop in a reasonably nice area of Brooklyn, not far from Anthony's office, which was home to several similar shops as well.

When relations between the families of Benoit Bovary and Anthony McReynolds began to transcend the sphere of business and develop into something more personal, Benoit would bring his young Emma for a visit to the McReynolds's lovely home in Greenwich, Connecticut, which Anthony had bought a few years after establishing his law practice.

Emma was presented to Julia (who she didn't like, not even a bit) and the young Philip, by that time ten years old.

"This is the little Monsieur McReynolds," Benoit smiled, pointing to Philip, who tried his best to hide behind a dresser and refused to come closer than ten feet to sixteen-year-old Emmanuelle Bovary. His eyes were full of fear and bewilderment, like a hare meeting a hawk.

"Philip, what the hell is wrong with you?" asked Anthony, feeling embarrassed and disappointed with his son's behavior.

On one occasion, Anna Ratajczik, Julia's closest friend, was also introduced to Benoit and young Emma. Anna brought her son Henry to be introduced. He was the same age as Philip, but his nature completely the opposite. While Philip was terrified, the young, precocious Henry tried to kiss Emma on the cheek.

*I like this little guy,* thought Anthony. *He's got some balls.*

Henry was bold — courageous, in fact. Anthony had decided long before that his son was too feminine, nowhere near man enough to be called his son. *Shy, scared and always crying,* thought Anthony. Emma's opinion about Philip, on the other hand, was complicated. It was as if he was perpetually anticipating some sort of misfortune. In that regard, Emma was quite sympathetic, seeming like a typical, caring older sister to the lanky Philip.

*"Semble qu'il prédit quelque disgrace."*

✕

In truth, Philip wished more than anything, during the few years that he was frequently around Emma, that he were ten years older, or at least like the older boys, who tripped over each other, bringing treats and compliments to the "French girl with the curly hair." However, it remained only a dream. To make things even more complicated, for Emma, routine was the worst poison. Just when she managed to get used to a location, she would get an itch to pull up stakes and relocate.

Still, it didn't take long until even all of the greater New York City seemed too small, and five years after returning to New York, when she turned 21, she departed for a life of traveling and adventure, wandering through across Europe, through both Central and South America, and even to locations in Asia and Australia.

The fifteen-year-old Philip cried hard the night before her departure for Paris. She tried to hug him in the airport, but out of a sort of automatic impulse, he shied away. Emma then told him she wouldn't be away for long.

However, she never returned. At first she wrote letters to Philip, her father and to some of her friends, but after a while it seemed that the wonders her eyes witnessed around the globe kept her too busy to write. Finally, the letters ceased entirely.

Philip dreamed for years of his "Madame Bovary." On many lonely nights, he dreamt of being held in her arms.

✕

Benoit, shortly after returning to New York City, had acquired a storefront in Brooklyn that became the new location of Bovary Antiquities. For various reasons, it had seemed to be a great location. Fate, however, has a sense of humor, and soon the neighborhood descended into crime, and soon was many a crack dealer's best known address.

Behind the literary cafe, a brothel went in — Eros Massage Therapy, it was called — and near many of the other antique shops sprang up taverns and bars. These taverns quickly became decrepit facilities, since they weren't especially elegant to begin with, with the regulars going into the streets drunk and spending hours sitting on the stoops of closed shops, sharing bottles of whiskey, scotch and rum that they purchased with coins scraped together each day.

There was noise throughout the afternoons, a general uproar and loud, bad music. From 4 PM onward, it was quite a challenge to pass by the pubs. The drunks gathered in groups and often threw bottles at passersby.

It was rumored that the pubs were controlled by some form of organized crime. Since many of the pubs were owned by Chinese immigrants who generally didn't speak a word of English, many equated that with the so-called Chinese mafia.

Every night, it seemed the gates of Hell opened in all their splendor. Drunks crowded the neighborhood, dominating the entire area and dragging chairs and tables in front of the various antique stores. They would drum on the tables, shouting, and singing along with the blaring music.

In extreme cases, having extended the festivities until seven or eight in the morning, the proprietors of the antique shops were forced to call the police. Even on nights when nothing extraordinary happened, the next day it was always necessary to hose down the sidewalks to clean up the beer and rum, and other liquids — sometimes including vomit and urine. This routine was known to everyone.

Among those who objected to this behavior, however, was Philip, who sought refuge from the grim experience of dealing with his mother by hanging out at Bovary Antiques.

It was a relatively small shop, although full of exquisite items, the like of which were found nowhere else in Brooklyn.

Benoit kept deep bonds of friendship with Fausto Muñoz, the owner of the shop next door, and when Anthony McReynolds's growing law practice took away his time and attention, Muñoz became Benoit's challenger for endless chess matches.

Not long after Emma's departure, Benoit had learned of an open storefront in Garden City, about ten miles to the east, and seized on the opportunity.

***

## 2014

Time went by, and in part due to financial problems and, some claimed, his daughter's distance, Benoit's health went sour. Less than three years had gone by when he was diagnosed with a heart condition. Upon learning of her father's diagnosis, Emma rushed back, but it was too late. Benoit passed away six hours before her plane touched down at JFK.

Emma wished there was a way she could avoid attending the funeral, but she knew that would be impossible. Anthony offered her a ride in the family's car, and she promptly accepted. Inside the car were Julia, with her usual antipathy, and Philip.

*He's grown a lot,* thought Emma. Still a boy in his face and traits, but very nearly the size of a grown man. Philip was at that time eighteen years old.

The burial was a quiet ceremony with only a few in attendance. Muñoz was unable to attend, as his doctor feared the stress would likely cause him to join his friend.

Emma eyes overflowed with tears, but still no sound came forth from her mouth. Julia was only there out of duty, as her marriage to Anthony was near its breaking point. The jaded Anthony no longer cared very much either, and was distracted by the thought of the caseload — among other things — waiting for him at the office. Every minute he spent at the cemetery meant fees that he was missing out on. The both of them were distracted by the protracted, hostile separation that they were going through. It was only for the sake of their old friend Benoit that they were putting on a good face and pretending that they were an intact family.

Anthony had picked Julia and Philip up at their Brooklyn apartment; Anthony himself was still living in the Greenwich house part of the time and staying at his office the rest of the time.

Philip was the only one who really cared about why they were at the funeral. Emma was standing there, so frail, so unprotected; Philip wished he were older, more secure, wiser.

He wished he could take her in his arms and whisper into her ear, telling her that everything would be all right. But he was only a teenager, and Emma Bovary was a grown woman. The only thing he did was to give her a tender glance and smile, followed by a brief hug, still long enough to imbue Fleur de Cabotine deep in his clothes. Emma placed her delicate lips upon his cheek and gave him a kiss — not a lover's kiss, but a tender, slow kiss on the cheek, and when she removed her lips from his face, it didn't make a sound.

Philip felt shivers. Emma's sweet breath was now so close to his mouth. An inch to the left and they would end up sharing a genuine kiss. He berated himself — how could he feel such things during her father's funeral? It was unacceptable even to his hormone-fueled teenaged mind. Philip tried to distract himself by focusing on Emma's sad eyes. Again it didn't work. They were so moist and beautiful, brimming with tears. Deep, like the ocean; prone to drown any careless soul. Rain began to fall, and those few seconds felt like a lifetime.

Still, it didn't last long. Anthony came to Emma to pay his respects, and apologized for being forced to leave sooner than expected. Julia, as always, proudly followed her husband. Philip wanted to stay, but the little courage he had left was now gone after a look from his mother's piercing eyes. Emma stayed, sitting by her father's grave for hours.

As the car pulled out of the graveyard, Julia said something about how sorry she felt for Emma's loss, ignoring the fact that disgrace was already knocking at her own door.

Several days had passed since Philip's brief encounter with Emma. As usual, he was alone in his room. It was a typical young man's room, with cardboard boxes stacked everywhere, having never been unpacked since he and his mother moved from Greenwich. The boxes were filled with toy cars with which he had long since lost interest and posters for video games that he had long since quit playing, but the emotions of a young man ran untamed through his veins. For the first time, he'd been in contact with a real woman and now his desire felt like a raging sea, prone to tear him apart. Philip sat on his bed and gathered a handful of sheets in his hands. His wrist still smelled of Fleur de Cabotine where he had grasped her arm. Ever since the funeral, Philip avoided washing that particular part of his body in order to avoid losing that scent.

It wasn't hard to imagine Emma right there with him. He was so used to being alone, to spending long, restless nights sweating in the summer heat, wishing for a female body to warm his own. In such moments, he could almost taste the sweet, sometimes salty flavor of a woman's kiss.

Philip lay down and began to let his fantasies take over. What would Emma's kiss taste like? Cherry? Strawberry? Peach? Philip decided on cherry. Those lips should taste like they looked. Emma would be there, standing in front of him. She would wear fishnet stockings and a corset, both black — nothing more... The thought of her bare pubic area gave him goosebumps. Did she shave it? Wax it? Keep it natural, or trim it a little? So many possibilities. He found that he could reach his climax simply by imagining what Emma's pubic hair was like.

He felt terribly guilty for thinking of her in such terms on an evening like this. He knew it was wrong, but still, it felt so good — a kind of bittersweet pleasure. Philip couldn't help himself — he needed to go on with his fantasy, and in his dreams, Emma was already on top of him. unbuttoning his shirt with those delicate hands of hers. Emma's lips searched frantically for Philip's, their tongues entwining in desperate kisses — wet, passionate kisses. Emma's lips soon departed from Philip's and now he imagined she was at his ears, gently biting the lobes. His body would shiver and tremble at every kiss, making her know she was following the right path. Now Philip's shirt was fully open, revealing his chest, and Emma would scratch at it passionately, playing with his nipples, running the tip of her index finger over them, making circles, smiling at every moan he uttered.

"Emma... it feels so good..."

"Want me to go on...?"

"...yes... please..."

Emma would whisper in his ear, kissing it right after while she trailed her fingernails down his stomach, all the way down. Philip squeezed the mattress when Emma's hand touched and then grabbed him through his trousers. It felt like walking though the stars. The tip was already wet, and her hand slid up and down, up and down. At this point Philip couldn't speak, only moan, keeping his eyes closed and mouth open. His left hand reached for Emma's, but she wouldn't allow him to entwine his fingers with hers, instead gripping his wrist, keeping his hand away.

Emma's other hand kept caressing Philip, now out of his trousers. Up and down, up and down, each time faster and harder, and more and more slippery. Philp wouldn't be able to hold himself back any longer and soon his whole body would stretch, and with a long moan, he would explode in Emma's hand, covering his trousers, his sheets and mattress. He would linger there for a while, eyes closed, refusing to let go of his fantasy and accept that it was never Emma's or any other girl's hand touching him. Outside, the rain was still falling.

✕

Emma felt a crushing weight of guilt for not staying close to her father when he was dying, for not being able to hold his hand tightly and say how much she loved him. How distracted she'd become, seeing so many sights! Madrid, Paris, Rome, Cairo, Mumbai, Bangkok, Hong Kong, Tokyo…

Now, having come back to the place her father had adopted as his home, there was no landscape from Spain to Japan beautiful enough to ease her pain.

By now, Muñoz was taking pills by the handful and drinking wine by the liter to help him cope with the loss, and to be able to help Emma with her own grief in a more bearable way.

"What are you planning to do from now on, *niña?*" asked Muñoz with a very rare tender tone in his voice.

Emma said nothing, but her eyes said everything. She didn't know what to do. She was no antiques dealer, and more importantly, the shop was filled with memories. She knew that if she sat down for long enough, she would begin to expect her father to come and embrace her, even knowing he was dead. Emma wouldn't be able to pick up where her father left off. Keeping the shop open would be an invitation to madness.

"I don't think it would be a good idea for you to try to run the shop, Emma... I really don't think so."

Emma sat silently.

"Nor it would be good to keep it closed."

Again not a single word came from Emma's lips, but her hazel eyes spoke. "Help me," they were crying to Muñoz.

"I could run it for a while. Until we, somehow, figure out what to do next."

"Oh, *merci! Merci!*" replied Emma.

"It is not a problem, niña, not a problem at all. I have a man who can run my place, and I will come to Garden City and take care of things for you for as long as is necessary. Now, have you decided where you are going to stay?"

"I'm not planning to stay for long."

"Still, while the inventory is opened, it would take a few months."

"No longer than that, then."

"I have an apartment not far from here, in Brooklyn, in a fairly good neighborhood, a safe one. Much better than where the old shop was. It was put up for sale, but people around here are not in the buying mood. There is furniture, everything."

"I'm not sure if I could accept it…"

"Don't take it as a favor. You would help me a lot by renting it. Some extra *plata* is always welcome."

✕

Even in the new apartment, being alone with her own thoughts and memories was the worst of all possible tortures. In order to keep her sanity, Emma decided to go to work for the owner of a small language school few blocks away from her apartment, a gentle, retired widow named Andrea.

The school was extremely small, no more than a couple of rooms. The first was a reception area and the other was used as the classroom. The reception area was limited to a couch and a counter. On the wall, a picture of the Eiffel Tower was hanging. "We've got to arouse the traveling mood in them… and you know what, the students will be pleased by having a French teacher," said Andrea with a smile. Emma smiled. That little lady, she could tell, was a fierce businesswoman.

The space where the lessons would take place was adorned with objects having to do with France, most having been brought by Andrea from her countless travels and a handful by Emma herself. There were eight tables arranged in a circle, a whiteboard, a video player, a small stereo system and a relatively large flat-screen TV. Andrea also tried to make the students feel at home by serving cookies and coffee at the end of the lessons. Again, a very successful idea.

Unlike the famous language schools — usually those that catered to immigrants who needed English lessons, where students were mostly noisy young people, at Andrea's school the ones taking lessons were often retired people and hotel employees. More than that, Andrea had the habit of avoiding the kind of rowdy students by politely saying, "Sorry to say, but we have no open courses now," in the very few times she came across an annoying teenager who wished to enroll. After a while, that became her main rule: No One Under 18 Permitted.

# 7: JULIA

Julia Rice was born in 1962 and grew up in Queens. Her father was a factory worker and her mother a seamstress. She grew up in a typically large Catholic household — she was the second youngest of seven children; three brothers and four sisters.

Her oldest brother, Richard, was born in 1952. Upon his graduation from high school in 1970, he enlisted in the Navy and became an F-4 pilot. He was deployed to Vietnam in 1972. His plane was hit by a North Vietnamese surface-to-air missile six weeks after his first combat mission and he was killed.

Julia was deeply impacted by the loss of her brother. She seemed to withdraw from life in general, and became something of a recluse. She didn't want to participate in school activities; she never hung out with her friends; even when the whole family went to the movies, something that was a big deal in their family while she was growing up, Julia didn't want to go, coming up with some excuse to stay home.

On the first day of eighth grade, things seemed to change. Julia met Anna Gibson. The two girls seemed to hit it off, and soon they were fast friends. There was something about Anna that took the sorrow out of Julia. It was like seeing a dried up rose come blossoming back into vibrant life.

After graduating from high school in 1981, Julia enrolled at Brooklyn College as an Art major, while Anna decided to attend

Virginia Tech. They stayed in touch, however, as close friends do. Anna worked part-time during most of her college years, usually carrying only six or eight hours' worth of classes.

On the last day of the spring semester in 1986, Julia was coaxed into going out on the town and wound up at a tavern on 9th avenue called Rudy's. There she met a tall, well-built fellow who was introduced to her as Tony.

Soon the two were sitting at a corner table talking quietly. "I really prefer to be called Anthony. Seems a little more mature, you know?"

They exchanged numbers, and the infatuation they found that night turned into more. Soon they were seeing each other regularly. Anthony got a position as a clerk for a district judge in Brooklyn. He was there for a year; following that he was an associate at a mid-sized lawfirm in Queens. Finally, he founded his law practice in 1990.

At last, they decided it was time to tie the knot, and Anthony and Julia got married in 1995. Anna Gibson Ratajczik, herself a newlywed, was proud to serve as Julia's matron of honor.

For the next twenty-one years, other than Anthony going to his office or the three days Julia spent in the hospital after Philip was born in 1997, Anthony and Julia were rarely apart.

# 8: H&P, INCORPORATED, PART I

## *2008*

"I could get addicted to this, man," laughed one of the gang of boys gathered around while pressing the sole of his foot against Henry's face.

"Goddamn it, Cody! You're gonna crush his skull doin' that shit," said another one of the boys. "You got to take it a little easier... be a little bit more subtle if you want 'im to survive to give you his lunch money *tomorrow.*"

By the tone in his voice and the respect shown on the faces of the others, it wasn't hard to realize that he was the leader.

"Sorry, man, but this fucker put up one hell of a fight."

"I know, next time you get to mess with him some more," said the leader, running the sole of his boot over the face of the second boy, who was also lying on the ground. "Now, *this* one wouldn't fight back even if I was holding his momma at gunpoint."

The two boys went downstairs into the school's basement where the locker rooms were located, dirty and bruised, and fervently hoping that no one would see them in this condition.

"Fuck you, man. We should have fought back!" muttered Henry.

"Oh, sure. And get beaten twice as bad?" replied Philip in an irritatingly cool manner. "You know better than I do that we wouldn't stand a chance against those guys."

"So what do we do? Just keep putting up with it? Keep on getting bullied?"

"It could have been worse."

"Like what? Getting gang raped?"

"That'd be one possibility, I suppose, but last week that guy took a dump on a pizza and forced three guys to eat it."

"God *damn!*"

"Don't worry. They'll get what's coming to them... one of these days. We'll make sure of it."

"So... a pact?"

"Pact?"

"Yeah. You know, an agreement."

"Like our own little company?"

"Yeah."

"Okay," said Philip. "Shake on it." He held out his hand.

"Done." Henry clasped hands with Henry, and a lifelong friendship was born.

# 9: THE ANTIQUES QUARTER

## *Present*

Although they may not have been major players in the business world, it seemed as if the antiques business of years ago had been much more profitable than it was today, particularly in the large cities. Now it seemed that only a few dealers remained, and only a handful of viable customers.

The older locals in Garden City tended to linger in front of the shop windows of the various antique stores, as they passed by. Even when they weren't really in the market or had no funds to make a purchase, but were simply window shopping, enjoying the opportunity to see some dusty, rusty objects that used to be part of their daily routine "back in the day" was enjoyable. It reminded them of a simpler time when there was no Internet, no cell phones, no satellite TV; happier times, the dawn of their long-departed youth.

But apart from those old-timers, the majority of the non-antiquing aficionados on the street didn't even glance at the shop windows; the dusty portals to yesterday were less noticeable than the autumn leaves blowing down the road.

This lack of customers was likely due in part to the exorbitant price tags on some of the items within; the cost of certain of the paintings, vases and even small figurines displayed in the late Monsieur Bovary's shop easily surpassed the monthly budget for a family of six.

The second factor driving the near-bankruptcy of his antique business was, at least in part, cultural: in many of the larger cities in America, most people wanted new things; it was no wonder there was little interest in a 200-year-old ivory statue or an 18th century oil painting.

Everyone was steadily riding a constant and torrid flow into the future. In the city, there was little room for the past, or for anything that was old. Yesterday was gone, too; it was old news and should be forgotten, lost in the dust of time. Still, there was a spark of hope for those who worshiped the past. Ironically, it was located in the small town of Garden City and other towns like it. Within this magical area were located more than 30 antique shops, two literary cafés, a book and record store, a glassblowing studio, and more. It was a real cultural relief for those chosen few who were devotees to things from the past.

In contrast, the less desirable element of society had successfully found a niche in the neighborhood where Emma was living, their success being an abundant source of endless trouble. There was noise throughout the day, frequent uproars from drunks gathered at the worst kind of bars nearby, and plenty of bad music.

Starting at about 6:00 PM every weekday evening, the doors opened, displaying temptations in all their splendor. The drunken crowd multiplied like the loaves and the fishes and spilled into the street until the revelers dominated the entire place. To the residents, there was nothing left to do but pray to a pantheon of diverse gods to have mercy on them until the next morning.

# 10: THE INTERNET CAFÉ

Badi Al-Hamadani was a remarkably large Iranian immigrant with an angular face and a long, thick beard. He wore a taqiyah on his completely bald head. He had the usual language difficulties when speaking his adopted English tongue, especially with verbs and prepositions, but nothing that prevented him from being fully understood. Despite being quite physically intimidating, he was extremely gentle and kind to people from any race, gender, and age, though he often displayed a slightly gentler demeanor while dealing with the fairer sex.

Philip had been Badi's first customer on the day that he inaugurated his establishment some six months before. The Around The World Internet Café was a small shop with diffuse lighting, filled with older and rather slow computers which Badi had bought secondhand, and uncomfortable chairs that he'd purchased at the liquidation sale of a failed business startup. The storefront was totally glass. Despite these structural problems, Badi was perpetually smiling behind his countertop.

✕

"You are addicted to the Internet, Philip."

Philip shrugged. "Yeah, I really think I am. It's like crack," he said, much to Badi's amusement. "I didn't think you were listening."

"Well, I can say that for good or for bad, I listen to a lot more than people think," Badi replied. "Your father has money, Philip. Why do not you have your own computer, at home? Bound to be newer and faster than these."

"I did," Philip replied. "A nice laptop. But my father threw it across the room a few months back when we argued. It's just a piece of junk now." The older man nodded. He had heard tales of the senior McReynolds's temper.

It didn't matter. Anything that meant Philip could spend a few more hours away from home was like opium to Philip. His addiction was most evident when he was checking his accounts on the social networking sites: Facebook, Twitter, and the rest.

# 11: WORK, WORK

If pain had a name, so would annoyance; It was Arthur Keller, or more specifically, the Keller Real Estate Office. It was the only place in the area where Philip had been able to find a job. The office was run by Arthur himself, a not-so-successful former real estate mogul now forced to work with rentals and tenants. By this time, it took Arthur half the year to earn what he used to bring in in a single month in the long-gone glory days.

Despite this, he kept up his pompous demeanor, ruling his tiny office with an iron hand. Arthur always wore a suit and tie, never repeating the same combination twice. According to an office urban legend, Arthur bought a suit and a tie for every one of the girls in the office that he'd sex with and then dumped. If that were the case, the odds would probably be on his side, because Arthur actually was the tall and handsome type, despite being in his mid-fifties. So tall, in fact, that being in the office often made him feel claustrophobic. Even for a short man, the office he occupied was tiny.

At the front desk, the office secretary — currently an older woman named Pearline — redirected the many unwanted visitors as rapidly as possible. To the very few who meant business, she was all tenderness.

"Would you like some coffee, sir/ma'am/miss? It's just freshly made," she would say.

After the coffee, Pauline guided the visitors down the sacred path between a massive set of shelves and a bank of glass windows to the inner sanctum where they finally would be able to speak with the majesty himself: Arthur, with his impossibly flawless, combed back silver mane of hair.

Arthur showed no mercy to those who were unable to bring him real business, as well to anyone in a minimum wage job. He would also often express disdain towards his employees, generally making a handful of them leave their jobs each month, some of them — especially the young women —in tears. Yet he restrained his behavior when dealing with Philip, arousing in the others feelings of both puzzlement and envy.

As a matter of fact, to Arthur, humiliating people whom he considered to be of a lower social strata was both an obligation and a right. And while many would do their best to escape duty, none would ever give up a right.

Philip was never mistreated, but his duties were quite humdrum and he often felt as though he was drowning in boredom. His routine always began at 7:30 AM. First he had to make coffee, and then check the morning's mail. After that, he checked every aspect of the office operations, from payments to the wax on the floor. Finally, it was also his duty to close the office; Arthur was to stay until 5 PM. He waited half an hour, and then, after checking to make sure everything was secure, Philip locked the shop and headed home.

At the end of the workday, Philip was witness to the sometimes hilarious, sometimes depressing and always grotesque performances of the drunks in the streets as he passed near the former Bovary's location in the antiques district.

Sometimes there were also women, wearing clothes so tight and low-cut as to leave nothing whatsoever to the imagination. They often seemed to be drunk, although their drunkenness was questionable, since they still avoided the eager, grasping hands of the other regulars. These women were employees of a neighboring establishment called "Eros Massage Therapy." Sure, there were massages available, but also many other services, depending on how much the customer was prepared to pay, and for those who were willing to pay an extra fee, there was the possibility of a "Happy Ending."

That beautiful Happy Ending. Despite the hefty price tag, there was a waiting list for those who needed this "therapy." It said something that Mr. Arthur Keller, who happened to be the owner of the building where Eros was located, was a frequent customer. He was, in fact, a card-carrying member of their point system: after five massages, the sixth was free. Only the "Happy Ending" fee would be charged. And with the 50 percent discount that he had negotiated as the business's landlord, it was even more appealing.

Philip, as much as he tried to deny it, had a burning curiosity about the brothel. Each time he ran across one of those women, his heart would bump and his hands and legs would shake. The ladies always noticed and had fun teasing the poor boy. On one occasion, a lady from the brothel brushed her lips across the nape of Philip's neck, making him shiver and nearly inducing a fever, his face turning a bright red.

Philip had sometimes — much more often than he cared to admit — been very curious about the services of Eros. But in addition to not having the means to pay for them, he had the conviction that he should remain "untouched" until the moment he found the right person. This line of reasoning was so overly romantic that it made his oldest childhood friend practically collapse to the ground with laughter upon hearing it. "D'you want your princess astride a white horse, too?!" Henry had said, barely able to speak, choking and tears pouring from his eyes. "Or how about if she rides *you* instead?"

"Oh, fuck *off,*" answered Philip, affecting an irritation that seemed almost feminine in Henry's eyes and made him laugh even more. There were men willing to do anything to satisfy their most basic needs. Philip, although he felt consumed by flames during the lonely nights, took pride in not being part of that group... or at least believing that he was not.

Philip never cared very much for the word 'relationship.' He felt it attempted to describe, in generic and sterile terms, romantic love, which was — or at least *should* be — wide and deep, all-encompassing. Such a deep love should last for a lifetime and even make people virtually godlike, as they could, together, produce a new life.

Still, Philip always ended up scolding himself for the romantic way in which he viewed the world, as his behavior never came to any sort of fruition. Despite his gentle ways and good intentions, Philip continually remained alone.

"You gotta dance according to the music being played," Henry had said to Philip on more than one occasion.

Philip always replied immediately and with rock steady conviction, "I never learned to dance." But now his convictions weren't so steady.

*Let us help you find your soul mate* was the promise made by practically every dating site on the Internet. There were a number of these where Philip kept an active profile. All of them offered a wide range of services such as the possibility of including up to six photos in his profile and a program that searched for the most likely match for his profile according to the answers provided on a questionnaire. Philip thought of most of the services as a scam, but what was really thrilling for him was the possibility of finding someone to spend some time with, someone other than his own shadow while walking aimlessly or at the office. Someone who would laugh at his ridiculous jokes and wouldn't succumb to boredom while Philip spoke for hours about the paradoxes between Greek myth and the pagan religions.

Hanging by a tiny thread of hope, Philip spent many hours trying to find a girlfriend. Apart from that, every hour that he spent at Badi's shop delayed the saddest part of Philip's routine: the journey back home. Along with the unpleasantness of sharing the company of his mother, Philip had to walk the darkened streets as he headed back home. Every night it seemed longer and more dangerous; as the streets were especially dark at night due to the poor lighting and the crack dealers were always around.

There were also tall trees with thick trunks and branches bent on both sides of one of the streets. The place was so dark that Philip refused to pass through this neighborhood as a child. At the time, he firmly believed that bloodthirsty vampires would stalk him from the tops of those sinister trees, ready to jump on the neck of the first careless soul who would cross their path.

Still, if the vampires were the only thing Philip had feared as a child, it would have been much more bearable to his parents. But during his childhood, Philip feared almost everything… or more like everything. He refused to wait for the elevator in the building corridor by himself. Sleeping alone was something utterly out of the question. Philip feared demons, witches, werewolves, psychotic living dolls, aliens as well as the aforementioned vampires.

Throughout his childhood, Philip had suffered from night terrors. Waking up startled during the night, screaming aloud and waking up the whole floor of the apartments in the process. Neighbors began to believe that Philip was being beaten by his parents during the night and some of them even considered the possibility that Philip was a victim of demonic possession.

Anthony's wealth was growing by this time, and yet a good night's sleep was something he would have paid any sum of money to have. He slapped Philip a few times out of frustration, and when this resort proved useless, he finally agreed to sending fourteen-year-old Philip to a psychologist.

"This boy needs to participate in some kind of sports," said the doctor. "In this part of his life, he has a lot of energy. If he doesn't spend all of it during the day, things like these night terrors can be very common."

Julia agreed with a nod. "I understand, Doctor."

The doctor looked straight into Philip's eyes but spoke to Julia: "I'm sorry if I'm being invasive, but does the boy have a good relationship with his father? I mean, does your husband talk to him? Participate in his life?"

Philip looked at the doctor with eager eyes, seizing on an extremely rare opportunity. Perhaps this gentle doctor could advise Anthony and Julia, but mainly Anthony, not to be so hard on him. Philip tried to speak, but Julia gave him a slight pinch on the arm and looked at him with a severe look on her face, then smiled at the doctor.

The doctor looked at Philip as if he already knew every word the boy had been about to say and felt sorry for him.

✕

Outside the doctor's office, Julia wasted no time in expressing her displeasure. "What kind of nonsense were you about to say to the doctor, Philip? Oh Philip, you're so unfair!

Your father and I love you so much… we just want the best for you, and *that's* how you repay us? Trying to embarrass us before a *stranger?"*

Philip tried to argue, but was immediately stopped by Julia, her eyes filled with tears. "Oh, Philip, you're *so* ungrateful!"

Anthony had driven them over and was waiting impatiently, smoking one cigarette after another while standing by the front fender of the sleek black car. In truth, there was no need for Philip to verbalize the fact that his father was rude and disinterested; his absence during the consultation had made the doctor immediately realize the nature of the relationship Anthony had with his son.

Julia got Philip settled in the back seat, her frustration boiling out of her, causing her to grip Philip's arm tightly enough to cause Philip to cry out in pain, which irritated his father even more.

Anthony thought it was all nonsense, and an unnecessary expense "This kid thinks money grows like weeds."

Philip was considered a "loser" by his father, even at an early age. His weakness was considered remarkable. Surely he would be a failure when he grew to adulthood. No doubt about it, according to Anthony. Julia was always tempted to agree with everything Anthony said.

He was always harsh with his son on the rare occasions that he spoke to Philip.

"What's the matter with you, Philip?! You're already a man and still afraid of things that don't even exist!"

Julia tried to ease the situation every time she saw that Philip was near his breaking point.

"Your father may seem harsh, but he loves you and cares about you. He cares about both of us. To your father, his wife and son are the two most important things in the world!"

And how was Philip's first kiss? According to what he imagined, it should had been very deep, very meaningful and dramatic. Most likely in the rain, after a fight with some pretty girl over some very silly little thing (in fact, a way to disguise their feelings for each other), or even after an ultimatum given by Philip to that special person who refused to accept the passion linking them…

The things Philip imagined about what that moment would be like were many and varied. However, none of them had ever come true. Instead, his first kiss was at fourteen at a school function, with a girl whose name he didn't even know. She said nothing and wasted no time. Philip felt so dizzy that he won the nickname of "Drooling Doggie" from Henry.

Still, the worst was yet to come. The next time they met, two days later, the girl rejected another kiss. Instead of hearing "I love you" or "I always loved you but never had the courage to say it" or even "I don't know how I could to live without you,"

Philip was told, "You've got really pretty eyes, but this was a mistake... sorry," and she walked away.

Philip nearly fainted, but as always, no one around, or at least no one who cared, even noticed. Except for Henry.

After hiding the chocolates and the rose in his bag, Philip had to hear the news from a laughing Henry that this girl had kissed every boy in their school from 9th grade to the senior class, and a considerable number of college men too. "You should be happy she didn't give you herpes!"

Philip felt even worse then. He had been eager to date a girl who would kiss anyone and then throw them away afterwards.

"I'm so *stupid,*" said Philip, rubbing his head. His eyes were filled with tears.

"Hey buddy! Don't be so hard on yourself. I thought of asking her out myself!"

"Really?" asked Philip with some hope in his moist eyes.

"Sure."

"And why are you keeping your left hand behind your back?"

Henry then showed him a pair of party invitations.

"Look at *this*... we're gonna have some *fun* Saturday night!"

Philip smiled for a brief moment and then shrugged. "I wish I could, but my Mom…"

Henry found himself, for once, at a loss for words. It wasn't enough for Philip to have problems at school; he also was forced to deal with Aunt Julia. Out of good ideas, Henry put his arm behind Philip's neck and made a proposal.

"Well, okay, then… let's pig out on the chocolate you were gonna give the serial kisser!"

# 12: H&P INCORPORATED, PART II

*2008*

The same gang of bullies showed up again a week or so after the first encounter. They began to harass Philip in a corridor at the school, pushing and smacking him around in a place where they knew no teachers would be likely to come along.

They had been tormenting Philip for several minutes when Henry came along.

"Hey!" he said. "Leave Philip alone!"

Their leader, a tall, dishwater blond kid named Alexander, laughed and said, "I guess you think you can make us."

"As a matter of fact," said Henry menacingly, "I am pretty sure I can." From his pocket he withdrew a long silver folding knife, the kind a fisherman might gut his catch with. He slowly opened it and held it with its blade pointing toward Alexander's belly. "I used to go fishing sometimes with my old man," he said. "He used to cut the guts out of catfish and perch and trout with this knife. If you don't get the fuck out of here right now, I'm prepared to do the same to you."

There was a long pause. Then one of the other boys, a fat ball of stupidity named Dean, spoke up.

"He ain't gonna do nothin."

Another second or three ticked away. Then Alexander blinked and said, "Come on." They all filed away muttering.

Henry folded the knife and handed it to Philip. "Put this away and keep it for me."

"Why?"

"I can't have it on me in case one of them decided to tell a teacher and they decide to search me."

"Oh, okay," said Philip. He unzipped his backpack and quickly slipped it inside one of its inner pockets.

# 13: EURYDICE

*2015*

Philip was headed to Badi's. While he appreciated the antiques displayed in the storefronts of the Antiques Quarter, Philip remembered something that his father had often said:

"A man can surely get down in the dumps, but when you go to the theatre by yourself, then you know you've hit rock bottom..."

Philip smiled. There were so many times that he had done exactly that, and his father had never realized it, or more probably, he'd never paid the slightest attention to Philip's activities nor his companions — as if he had any. Nor did Anthony know that Philip e-mailed himself from time to time with the excuse of needing to remind himself about important things. "The personification of failure," Anthony would certainly have said, had he known.

✕

Inside the store, Badi was entertaining a little boy by allowing him to climb on his outstretched arm. As his friend was very busy amusing both the child and his mother, who was very impressed with Badi's strength, Philip checked himself in to the first available computer and began to open a series of browser tabs, checking the various sites where he was a member, hoping for a new message. Much to his surprise, there was one, and a very interesting one at that: a girl who was into Greek mythology.

"I'm looking for my Orpheus, a man strong and brave enough to descend to the depths of Tartarus and rescue me from the darkness of my loneliness," was the sentence used by the girl to describe herself.

"That was deep," thought Philip with a smile, unexpected even to himself. This girl seemed so deep and so very poetic. Something Philip had sought for so long now was so close.

Philip continued to look over her profile, but nothing more about it caught his attention like that first sentence. He didn't care whether she was sixteen, seventeen, nineteen, nor if she was in high school or already in college. Not even the few pictures of her were worthy of anything more than a few glances. Her name was Eurydice; she was blonde and lean. That's all he really noticed.

For some unknown reason, a memory of Philip's wretched childhood came up while he was writing a reply to Eurydice: the day on which he'd had some money which Julia had given him to buy some things he had wanted, but instead he bought roses for Emma Bovary.

"White roses are more suitable, young gentleman," smiled the owner of the flower shop. "Giving her red ones might lead her to believe you're ready for a commitment."

"But I *am!*" replied Philip.

The owner was struck by so much naiveté and thought it was beautiful. "How old is your muse?"

"She's seventeen."

"Then you might have to wait for a few more years..." smiled the owner while finishing the flower arrangement. Philip's eyes flashed and he showed a smile that had rarely come out since then. Julia found out what he had done, and as one would expect, things went badly.

One day Julia, who had been harboring a cold dislike for the "overaged" French girl, as she thought of her after having seen seeing her initials within a heart design drawn by her son, took action. She decided that she would mock Philip as viciously as possible until he gave up all thoughts of being with that little slut.

"Oh, my poor little boy... shame on you...! I can't believe you are in love with this Emma, this filthy little French tramp."

Philip wouldn't say a word; as always, he was afraid of his mother.

"Oh, my poor child... you know nothing of life, of the real world, or what it's like out there... how can you possibly think you're in love at your age? Oh, Philip... how silly you are, my son... how ridiculous this all is..."

Julia spat a long string of pejorative and cynical sentences at Philip, many of them accompanied by giggles, and ultimately Philip fell on his knees in tears.

Julia then began to speak to him in soft and gentle tones, the same old strategy that she had used since he was just a small boy, and began to embrace and to comfort him, still treating him like the Little Philip.

"This horrible French girl... it's all *her* fault..."

It was *always* someone else's fault.

The mental image of his mother laughing at him was already gone by the time Philip sent a message to Eurydice. It was time to go home. When Philip was about to log off of the computer, another profile caught his attention. This one was for a Middle eastern or perhaps Asian girl with short hair and the saddest smile he had ever seen, even sadder than his own. Still, it was time to go to a place where sad and saddest were only empty words. Sadness had a name, and it was Julia.

✕

Eurydice had left a message with her phone number and the following message:

"I don't think you'll call me, but just in case, here's my number..."

It was obvious that she was putting up a barrier to prevent herself from being hurt. She was clearly the sort of girl who had

had some bad relationship experiences. Philip thought for a moment, then replied:

"I'll make you a deal: If I call you, we go out to a movie, I'll buy the popcorn and you will let me hold your hand..."

It was a silly bet. When he was just a child, Emma Bovary herself had made him the same promise when Philip was putting up a fuss about getting vaccinated for the German Measles many years before. "If you'll let them give you the shot, I will hold your hand during it and afterwards."

Once he finished sending the message, Philip took out his phone and made the call.

The phone rang once... twice...

"Hello?"

"Eurydice?"

"Who? Who are you calling for?" asked a male voice. Voices were audible in the background, and then the same voice said: "There's a guy on the phone who wants to talk to somebody named 'You-rid-uh-see?'" He carefully pronounced each syllable, breaking into laughter after saying the name.

"Oh, that's me!" came the reply from a young woman's voice, clearly trying to avoid laughing herself. Once she came to the phone, there came the question: "Are you my Orpheus?"

That first contact was a bit disappointing: It wasn't like Philip always felt attracted to introspective girls, but how could someone who felt comfortable surrounded by crowds of people feel attracted to the introverted, shy young man that Philip was?

Eurydice had a sweet voice, but spoke very quickly. "Can we meet tomorrow? I know a great old movie house. Can we?"

"Well, yeah… yeah, of course... what time would be good for you?"

Their meeting was scheduled for noon the next day. Then he wrote back to Eurydice, "I'm looking forward to meeting you. See you tomorrow."

The place they chose to meet was a medium-sized shopping plaza. It was closer to Eurydice's home, but a bit further from Philip's place, a golden rule in the book of Internet dating: the safety of female users was priority. Philip set out at 10:25 AM, fairly well dressed, at least by his standards: A blue shirt with grey stripes, and sleeves fashionably rolled up to the middle of his forerms, and a pair of jeans that were slightly faded. He wore a fairly good if inexpensive cologne; perhaps a bit too much. While she waited, Eurydice chewed no less than a dozen breath mints.

Being at the place where one was to meet his date a full hour in advance was not something that any of the many dating etiquette sites that Philip had perused necessarily recommended, but Philip couldn't help himself. His anxiety was running high. Thoughts kept rushing through his mind in flashes.

*Is this going to go well? Will she let me kiss her? Will she want to go on a second date?* He was so lost in thought that he didn't even notice when Eurydice arrived. After looking at him from a fair distance for a while, she approached him.

"Orpheus?"

Philip looked up, quite surprised, and saw Eurydice.

"You're Eurydice…?"

It turned out her real name was Maurina. She was ten times more beautiful in person, though Philip realized he hadn't paid very close attention to her photos on the website. She somehow reminded him of Emma. She was not at all the kind of girl you see on men's magazine covers, but to Philip she was irresistible. Long hair; nose, eyes and mouth so delicate that they seemingly would shatter if touched carelessly… her eyes were hazel, even more radiant in the sunlight. She was surely beautiful.

The movie wasn't scheduled to start until 6 PM. Philip and Maurina/Eurydice had arrived quite far in advance, so there was lots of time available. They found a table in the food court, which was just a few steps away from the theatre.

"Do you want a coffee?" asked Philip.

"No, just water is fine," said Maurina, adding, "The weather is a little hot for coffee."

That must have been a good sign. According to the websites, there were a number of foods that people should avoid consuming before kissing someone else. Coffee and tomato salad with onions headed the list.

Philip went to one of the food outlets, but when he returned to the table with two bottles of water, caught the first bad sign. Maurina looked him up and down as he was approaching, and the look on her face hinted that he didn't quite measure up to her expectations.

"I thought you were a little taller. You're about my height... how tall are you again?"

"I'm five foot nine," said Philip.

"No way!" Maurina laughed.

From that point on, Philip felt his hopes fading away. There was virtually no chance for a kiss, much less starting to date this girl regularly. Another bad sign was the silence that periodically fell between them, when neither of them would say a word for a while. The only sound was that of them sipping at their water.

It was Philip's nature to put too much emotional energy into his relationships. There were too many expectations; great expectations. The opportunities for a relationship were so few and so unlikely to become something good; therefore the end of such relationships were exponentially more painful.

Maurina kept a smile on her face; it was a smile that seemed false and uncomfortable and slightly cynical. According to Emma, there were only two kind of people who smiled all the time: fools or liars. Neither were very much appreciated, anywhere from Argentina to Japan. It didn't really matter who broke the silence; once the conversation resumed, there was no depth. Maurina said nothing, yet everything, regarding her former relationships, something that Philip also did not appreciate.

She told him all about her time at college, and narrated with excessive detail how the overly zealous mother of her ex-boyfriend used underhanded, systematic methods to separate them. Another bad sign. A *very* bad sign. Maurina had only praise for her former boyfriend, especially about his height. "This mall is very popular with his friends," she said.

*So why the hell did we come here? Maybe in the hopes that you'd see him?* thought Philip. The reason would have been obvious to even the most inattentive mind.

From that point on, Philip's consternation increased by a precipitous rate. In addition to no longer hoping that this meeting would bear fruit, Philip began to think of her easy and constant smile as disturbing. Philip was seriously considering leaving well before their movie was to begin, as soon as his first opportunity made its appearance, but it never came. 6 PM approached, and they made their way to the theater.

Some time passed without a word being said, nor any move made; they simply watched the movie in the most prosaic way. Midway through the film, Philip happened to glance over at Maurina and noticed she was staring at him with an unusual look on her face, as if she was saying, "Come and get it."

*What do I do now?* thought Philip.

Philip's hesitation was heightened by the nature of the look on Maurina's face. It wasn't a tender look, not passionate nor even mildly interested. It was as if she was saying, "So... are you just gonna sit there and do nothing?"

It was somehow a good sign. It had been a long, long time since Philip had felt a girl's lips pressed against his. Years, actually.

With the last of his remaining courage, Philip moved toward Maurina until their shoulders touched. He noticed that her breathing was slightly accelerated. He even had the impression that he could see her heartbeat slightly visible beneath her blouse. He placed his left arm behind her neck. Then he asked to hold her hand.

At that moment, Maurina seemed impatient. Philip felt as if he had gone too far too quickly by asking to hold her hand. Should he have asked her first if he could put his arm around her before he actually did it? In any case, the damage was already done.

"You've lost the bet," Philip said. Then he kissed her twice in a row, on the face, gradually approaching her delicate lips. Philip silently counted to five and finally took the leap of faith; he kissed her on the lips.

Bells began to chime inside his head. Maurina's lips were so warm and soft that it made a thousand chills run up and down his spine. It was heaven. He placed a hand on her cheek, wishing that that moment could last hours, if not forever.

*Some worthless day lost in the middle of 1979…*

*Dear Book that thinks of itself as a diary:*

*Let's talk about today… It had been pale and sad, and also unbearably boring.*

*I'm always alone… So alone. And as if that wasn't bad enough, my mother is always stalking me, always telling me what to do, when to do it and how to do it…*

*God, sometimes I just hate my mother.*

*Kasumi*

# 14: H&P INCORPORATED, PART III

*2008*

Several months had passed since the incident with the knife. Philip had mostly forgotten about it, and Alexander and his gang were mostly out of the picture; they had been caught by the school principal harassing another student, so they had been on their best behavior for several weeks, under the watchful eye of the administration and faculty.

One afternoon Philip was walking home alone; Henry had a doctor's appointment, and Julia was busy and couldn't pick him up.

About two blocks from home, he was surprised by Alexander. On this particular day, he was alone. Just as Philip was approaching a cellar entrance to a below ground apartment, Alexander stepped up out of the stairwell and said, "Well, well... look who's all by himself."

Despite the fact that he should have turned and run, Philip froze.

"Your little boyfriend ain't here today," sneered Alexander. "No one to protect you."

Philip dropped his backpack on the ground and fell to his knees. He unzipped the bag and began to fumble inside.

"Gonna find a book on how to fight me off, pretty boy?"

Just then, Philip found what he was looking for. He flipped the knife open and rose to his knees.

"Ooooooh, pretty boy's got a knife! What are you planning to do with that, p —"

Just at that moment, however, Philip swung the knife toward Alexander, mindlessly and angrily slashing the blade in an arc. The path of the swing would have intersected with the side of Alexander's chest. However, Alexander stumbled backward and seemed to suddenly disappear, tumbling backward down the stairs. There was a yelp and a thump, and then silence.

Philip stepped forward to the edge of the stairwell, and there was Alexander, motionless at the bottom of the stairs. His head and neck were at an odd angle, and there was a dark red pool of blood forming on the concrete underneath his head.

Philip knew what happened to kids who got in this kind of trouble. They got sent to reform school, and usually came out worse than they went in. He looked around and made sure no one was watching, then turned and headed home.

Alexander's body was discovered a day or two later. The NYPD nosed around the neighborhood for a few days, then attributed his death to a random mugging and filed it away.

# 15: SMELLS AND TASTES

*2015*

Philip was passing by Madame Bovary's store and was shocked to see it open.

*"Bon soir, Monsieur Philip,"* said Emmanuelle Bovary with a smile as Philip entered the doors of the antique shop. Philip was astonished. Emma was dressed in much more casual fashion than he was used to: a dark cotton shirt and grey yoga pants. No makeup, and that gorgeous, wavy hair of hers left unruly, some locks hanging over one eye, partially covering it, and even touching her soft lips.

*Why have I not gotten back in touch with her?* Philip wondered. The whole thing was so surreal. He had never seen Emma like this — so relaxed, seemingly as if they could have had some — even as friends — intimacy.

Suddenly Philip was distracted by an intense yet still delicate scent. What was it? Jasmine? He couldn't identify it. Just then, some soft music began to play nearby.

*"Bon soir, Mademoiselle Bovary."*

Emma smiled more broadly at Philip, making him feel even more uneasy. Then he recalled a rule he had been taught by his aunt Anna: be careful while addressing more mature women; don't be too formal, or they might think that you're treating them like an old lady. Especially women in their thirties or forties.

"Well," said Emma, still smiling. "Today there is not much to do in the shop itself, so we can move on to today's lesson if you like."

*Lesson? What lesson?* thought Philip. *And since when do I work here? And when did she begin to work with antiques?* Philip kept wondering, confused.

Emma came close to him, and looked at Philip carefully, finally asking him, "Philip, have you been drinking?"

"Drinking?" he burst out in surprise. "No! No! Of course not, I don't drink... I never have!" said Philip, feeling even more confused. But after a moment, he began to think about his fuzziness and inability to remember things such as how he got there, when he began to work for Emma, and a few other details. All of it could be easily explained in one short sentence: Philip was heavily drunk.

"Fausto gave you wine. Am I wrong?" Emma smiled.

"I... I don't remember!"

Emma's eyes were now tender, almost mothering. "It is okay, Philip. It's very common at your age." Then, coming close to him, she said, "To be honest, I think it's about time you began to behave like a young man of nineteen."

"Miss Bovary... I... I... uh..." Philip felt more anxious with each step Emma took towards him.

"Please, Philip... call me Emma," she said, touching his lips with her index finger, in a sort of "stop talking" gesture. By this time, Philip's heart was ready to burst. Her hazel eyes stared straight to his own. He was afraid; it seemed as if she could see straight through him. It couldn't be — Philip didn't want her to know what was going through her mind at that moment. But then Emma smiled mischievously, as if she could read his very thoughts.

"How about some coffee? It will help keep you from having a hell of a hangover."

Philip took a deep breath, his legs shaking, his whole body shivering. He closed his eyes for a moment, trying to ease his excitement. His heart was still pounding when he opened his eyes again and saw that Emma was standing face-to-face with him, their lips merely an inch apart.

*"Parfois, Philip, tout ce qu'une femme désire est de se sentir désiré."* ["Sometimes, Philip, all that a woman wants is to feel desired."]

Emma's soft, rosy lips touched Philip's, pressing to his tightly, almost hermetically…

\*\*\*

Philip woke up with a start, his body covered in sweat, with a thirst like that of a camel who had traveled for seven days across the Sahara.

*It was just a dream…* thought Philip. It had been a while since he had such a pleasant dream. The miseries of his daily life somehow became able to infiltrate his dreams, and for the first time in a long time, he had had a pure and lovely dream.

Loneliness tasted particularly bitter on that morning, and the taste was growing stronger by the second, making it beyond unbearable by the end of the day. Yet something of a balm was on its way. While heading home after locking up the office, Philip saw an impeccably well-dressed young woman with curly hair and a long linen scarf around her lean neck. It was Emma.

Since the funeral, he hadn't heard from her, being so wrapped up himself with his own family problems. He actually had thought that she would have been in France by now, but she wasn't. Emma Bovary was directly in front of him, and when she spotted Philip, she smiled a gorgeous smile.

"Philip!" said Emma, and he heard that unmistakable accent of hers. As she came closer, he caught the scent of Fleur de Cabotine.

"Emma…"

"Philip… it's been a while."

"Yeah, it sure has!"

"A lot has happened since the last time we saw each other," she said softly.

"Yeah, it has…"

"It's must be so difficult… it made me sad when I heard about the divorce, but to be really honest, somehow I was not really surprised."

"No, me either… it was more the way it happened … "

"Is your mother doing all right? I mean, despite of what has happened?"

"She's doing better now… Aunt Anna came up and kind of forced her to make some decisions."

"I am glad to know it. Do you have time for a coffee?"

Philip accepted promptly. How could he do otherwise? He had been craving to see Emma again for such a long time, and now the opportunity was there, presenting itself; he had to take advantage of it.

They spent a couple of hours chatting over coffee. Emma told Philip about the antique shop she had inherited, which she, thus far, had never had the courage to step into. So far she had been giving French lessons, and asked Philip to drop by at any time. They said their goodbyes, and she kissed him on the cheek. Philip then spent the next two days refusing to wash that spot on his face.

✕

*"Vous voulez apprendre le Français?"* "Still want to learn French?"

These were the final words that Emma had spoken to Philip before they parted. Philip, by this time, had grown more concerned about finding a girlfriend than anything else, but to get closer to Emma, he would have gladly taken lessons in Polish, in Arabic — hell, in Mandarin, if necessary. Thus it was that he went to one of Emma's classes, a free-of-charge trial lesson, as she advertised it.

Philip showed up shortly before 7 PM and sat down in the only empty seat. He tried to focus on the lesson itself, but he found himself continually captivated by the teacher rather than the teachings. Emma was simply gorgeous speaking her mother tongue. She was sexy and yet still so classy and elegant. Every word, every move, brought tiny electrical charges running over his skin, up and down, giving him goosebumps. Within minutes his imagination took him to a different place; now Emma was lying under him, while Philip held her wrists, both of them engulfed by bliss.

The lesson itself took nearly an hour, and toward the end, Philip began to realize that he didn't really fit in there. In a few months, he would gladly join the course, but something there felt suffocating to him. It was hard to say what, exactly; perhaps the classroom itself, or the other students — mostly retired ladies and a middle-aged, self-proclaimed Don Juan.

Philip's second date with Maurina was once again a disaster. Maurina didn't fall for him even after giving him what seemed like hundreds of passionate kisses, unleashing hurricanes of excitement within his mouth. It was just when he was ready for what he was sure was going to come next that she told him that she thought they should "just be friends."

"We don't have enough chemistry," she said. Philip shook his head. What did she want from him, the Periodic Table?

So there was Philip, once again being greeted by his old friend Badi, who was waiting with two cups of his famous hot chocolate. Too hot for the occasion, but Philip gladly accepted the offer anyway.

"An extra shot of energy for the girlfriend hunter," Badi said. He proposed a toast at a time when there was no reason to toast at all, at least not for Philip. Badi, on the other hand, had plenty of reasons to toast, as he was dating a curvaceous Argentine girl named Amelia.

"How was your last date?" asked Badi, already aware of how badly it must have gone simply by the expression on his young customer's face.

"It didn't work out so well, but it was kinda funny," Philip replied. After that, Badi left Philip to go and run an errand. He wanted to do so much more for the sad-looking boy, but he had his own burden to deal with.

Even with the little pride he had left badly wounded, Philip wasted no time and began his girlfriend search all over again. This time the dating site offered plenty of good opportunities.

The first girl who caught his attention was a blonde surfer from California. Her name was Melissa, but went by the name of Surfing Chick. She was 22 years old, and showed off her assets by wearing tiny bikinis in dozens of photographs. Philip felt as if she were way out of his league, but he figured, why not try? He sent her an introductory message.

The second girl he found, Amanda, seemed somewhat more promising. She was a 17-year-old girl of Japanese ancestry, with extremely delicate features, like a porcelain doll. She went by "Kawaii Girl" — "kawaii" being a Japanese term meaning "cute" or "adorable." When Philip first glanced at it, he misread it as "Haiku Girl" and wondered if she specialized in that form of poetry.

There was also a redhead called "Mary Jane" looking for her Spider-Man. Philip approached them both, but was most interested in Amanda. He was very attracted to her, even though she seemed to lack that something that would usually catch the attention of a male right away. It seemed that it was the combination of her black, straight hair, cut short, the permanently tanned tone of her skin, and the sadness in her eyes. He felt as though there was something strange about Amanda, but he couldn't quite place it, and it certainly didn't keep him from approaching her.

By the time Philip left Badi's internet cafe, Maurina was just a fading memory.

✕

Upon arriving back at his apartment building, Philip came across an unusual scene: the lights in the windows of the apartment were on and a figure could be seen through the curtain. Not only one, but *two*. One of them was smoking and walking from one side of the room to the other. Julia was awake.

*What's going on now?* thought Philip.

He climbed the stairs, trying to anticipate the argument that Julia would use to highlight her qualities as a perfect mother and accuse Philip of being a terribly ungrateful son. A few steps from the door, however, there was another surprise. Voices were coming from inside the apartment. Besides Julia's, Philip heard a man's voice, and that of another woman. The woman's voice was familiar to Philip.

"Julia, don't be silly. He's not coming back; you need to take him to court right away! Are you going to just go on, leaving things as they are?"

"He *will* come back to me, Anna. Anthony is just confused... tired. He still loves me..."

"How can you believe in such *crap,* Julia? If he loved you, he'd be here with you. With you and your *son.*"

Julia made no reply.

"You can't possibly be so blind. You weren't like this before, Julia. What's happened to you?"

Julia burst into tears, her cries breaking down into sobs as reality forced its way into her mind, the awful truth that effortlessly overpowered and obliterated her sweet illusions.

"Don't cry Mrs. McReynolds... I've seen cases much worse than yours," said the male voice, clearly trying to comfort Julia. She, however, was still in tears.

"It was all his fault... all *Philip's* fault... he's destroyed my marriage. Anthony said so many times, he tried to warn me..."

"For God's sake, Julia! It's not the boy's fault!" said Anna with a sigh.

And Philip sighed as well, losing all his will and desire to enter the apartment. Instead, he was trying to devise a way to get back to the street.

Aunt Anna, after concluding that Julia's inertia was hopeless, had hired a lawyer on her own. His name was Mark Keller, Attorney at Law. Along with Anna, he had come to Julia's apartment in an attempt to convince her that a divorce suit was her best choice, but so far, Anna's efforts had been fruitless. Julia continually blamed Philip and made excuses for Anthony's behavior.

*"Love was cruel and treacherous, like a nymph who lured unwary sailors, only to drag them to the bottom of a sea of tears…"*

# 16: THE CHINESE WHORE

Long marriages are likely to face some stormy weather, but Julia and Anthony's seemed to have more than its share. Frequently, they grew cold and distant from one another, even by Anthony's standards, and he was always a hard man. The environment of their home became suffocating, claustrophobic. Fights would start for trivial reasons and often escalated to alarming degrees.

Julia began to notice the change in her husband's mood.

"What's gotten into you, Anthony?"

"It's nothing, just some problems at the office. You don't need to worry."

Problems? Of what sort? Financial? That didn't seem to be the case. They were more prosperous than ever, having plenty of everything, ignoring completely the hardships that an ordinary worker would need to overcome to have met even their most basic needs. Philip was able to buy books at will, with no concern whatsoever of the cost.

Julia spent obscene amounts of money on designer clothing and at a nearby gym and even considered plastic surgery.

Anthony owned a closet full of suits in quantities enough for a lifetime, as well as the finest shoes, ties and blazers.

However, this abundance didn't make him a happy man. Surrounded by his wife and son, he felt as if he was in a prison.

He began to search for excuses to be away from home more and more. No longer was he capable of bearing the squeaky voice of Julia or the extravagances of his son. Suddenly, Julia looked ancient, with so many wrinkles on her face.

✕

"I don't have time now... leave me alone!" Anthony spat at Julia one day when she invited him to listen to a song they used to love when they were dating. Julia talked about singers who no longer performed, some of whom were already dead. They were both tied to the memories of a world that no longer existed. They were relics from a dead world.

However, Anthony still wanted to live, to feel young. He was eager to be part of this new world that had been formed right before his tired eyes. And to do so, he needed a guide: someone who would not be stuck in the past, but was living in the present. Anthony needed the company of someone young.

✕

At the age of 56, Anthony was still an attractive and vigorous man. He hadn't gone bald, nor become obese; he was taller than average and had an extremely good financial portfolio. He would have no difficulty in finding a young partner.

Anthony wasn't looking for any sort of serious relationship, just an adventure, as Julia was enough of an annoyance to him. Besides, even though he was weary of his householder's life, abandoning his wife and teenage son was unthinkable. How could he do such a terrible thing? Julia was so alienated, futile and naïve. She wouldn't have the ability to raise Philip by herself until he became a man. And poor Philip? His troubles were in a class of their own. As hysterical as his mother, lost in thick books, often unaware of the reality around him, but living in a dream world, regurgitating nonsense, often in endless monologues.

"Only a monster would leave this pair on their own," Anthony thought. He started dating young girls, some of them as young or even younger than Philip. Still he couldn't find fulfillment... until Laura came along.

✕

Laura Maeda was an Asian girl with mischievous eyes which were always adorned with elaborate makeup. She sported an elegant Cleopatra-like hairstyle. Even though she might have lacked the physical assets exhibited by Julia in her youth, Laura could be extremely seductive. Her gaze was wicked, even somewhat promiscuous. The shape of her full lips gave her a constant smile, cynical and challenging. She seemed to display an expression of constant sexual arousal. She had been working at Anthony's office for about three months, and despite the 30 years that separated her from her employer, she felt violently attracted to him.

20-year-old Laura Maeda was of Japanese and Thai ancestry; her parents had emigrated to the United States from Bangkok in 1993, and Laura was born just three years later.

She had recently broken up with a boyfriend of about her own age, and since that time she found her dating life frustrating. "So silly," she would say of her college mates and friends, to the point that she would only sleep with them to ease her urges. Never more than a one-night stand, however. There was nothing really interesting about them; they were of two types: muscular and dumb or bookish and insecure. Neither type really knew how to hold a woman. As her frustration was growing, Laura began to fantasize about a "real man," as she would say — someone strong, and at the same time, delicate. A man who knew how to treat a woman, in bed and out. And her boss, Anthony, seemed to be just that kind of man.

Anthony, on the other hand, despite being sick and tired of his wife, would not give in to her advances. Instead, he spoke to Laura only when strictly necessary, always addressing her as "Miss Maeda." before her name on the rare occasions he actually addressed her as anything other than "girl." But she began, slowly, to get under his skin. He found himself wondering how it would be to kiss her, what the scent of her skin was like. And then he began to imagine her lying in the bed. In Anthony's dreams, Laura's face would show a sort of suffering alongside pleasure, maybe even shedding a few tears.

✕

As time went by, Anthony's interest in Laura became more and more obvious. She began to take advantage of it, dressing in a much more provocative and revealing way. Anthony couldn't avoid feeling attracted by her demeanor. Laura was pure lust and debauchery. It was like the gateway to a magical world of pure delight for the senses. Laura grew more famished, only now just being watched by Anthony wasn't enough for her. She wanted physical contact with him and would take any little chance. While handing him a stack of documents, she would linger, touching his hand, looking straight into his eyes. The seasoned and experienced man felt his heartbeat pounding. He would tremble and sweat, still trying to hide such signs and failing miserably at it. Anthony was soon to be hers. It was only a matter of time — only a little time. And for Laura, nothing was more exciting than the feeling of being in control.

✕

Anthony's lust was soon to reach the breaking point, and each additional day that he couldn't bring his fantasies with Laura into the realm of reality made him sore and ill-humored. As for that, Philip and Julia bouncing around were beyond unbearable. Still, the father and husband would not allow himself to shy away from his obligation and forced himself to fulfill his duties. It was okay to endure his son's and wife's presence for a while. Only on the weekends, only two days. The rest of the week Anthony could see Laura. Just to be nearby, to see her, was enough. At least until a very unfortunate, or perhaps fortunate, morning.

✕

*2014*

Anthony and Julia were lying in bed after early morning sex. It was the "main course," as many would say, and, for both of them, not quite joyful, and, as always, instigated by Anthony. This time Julia didn't offer as much resistance as she sometimes did, nor insist on her usual set of rules — not in here, not like this, not at this pace — perhaps some sort of female intuition was warning her, but still she felt too secure at her position, in many ways, and the best she would do was not to refuse Anthony too much.

On the other hand, where most husbands might seek satisfaction, Anthony found just one more reason to be frustrated. Making love to Julia had become a savorless experience. She was numb, as always, and fell back asleep shortly afterwards, snoring within minutes. Anthony felt nothing but sadness; still, his lips displayed a slight smile as he caressed Julia's face. As much as she had aged, Julia was still beautiful. Amidst the wrinkles, the face of the cheerful young woman whom Anthony had met in college years was there.

*"The devil is in the details."*

The following morning, everything was the same as it had been for weeks: Philip burying his pockmarked face into some obscure book written by an unknown author about some silly matter. Julia talking pure nonsense about some sort of designer bag. Was it Gucci? Prada? Who gave a rat's ass? That was the real problem — Anthony didn't care anymore. Whatever his wife said came across to him like the buzzing of a mosquito.

*When did we distance ourselves from each other this much?* Anthony thought sadly.

He barely ate a thing, though Julia didn't notice; he only sipped some coffee. When he headed to the office, he tried to kiss her goodbye. He aimed for her lips, but involuntarily she turned her face, offering him her cheek. Anthony's attempt to share a kiss with his wife fell flat. A small gesture, which Julia didn't even notice, had sealed the fate of their marriage.

Settling into his office, Anthony felt overwhelmed, thinking of Julia while trying to cope with the rush of feelings he had for Laura. He sat contemplating, resting his chin on his thumbs. Deep inside, Anthony felt like a young man again, looking around at everything, desperately trying to find a glimmer of hope, trying to feel alive. He was praying, in his own way, for someone to save him. The prayers from this non-religious man were promptly answered: Laura came in, swinging her hips gently and looking him in the eye as if to say, "Come and get it..."

*This girl must be out of her mind...!* Anthony thought.

Laura wore a white skirt so tight that the outline of her tiny panties was clearly visible. Covering her upper body she wore a black silk blouse under which it was clear that she was wearing no bra. She kept looking straight towards Anthony, and her eyes took on an even more wicked gleam. For a few seconds he stood still as Laura approached.

"Here are the papers that you asked for last week. I'm sorry it took so long for me to locate them."

"Thank you very much, Laura," replied the astonished Anthony. It was the first time he had ever called her by her given name.

Laura saw her opportunity and bent forward over his desk. Anthony thought he saw a glimpse of one of her nipples and felt goosebumps spring up across his arms and shoulders. After leaving the papers on Anthony's desk, Laura walked slowly towards the door, and before leaving, looked over her shoulder at him, smiling slightly as he saw that his eyes were fixed firmly on her rounded ass.

Anthony was completely and utterly disturbed, possessed by an uncontrollable desire. His penis was pulsating, so rigid that it hurt. In one involuntary impulse, he touched himself and realized that his cock was slippery, his underwear already soaked by his fluids. He thought about masturbating right there at his desk. It would be so easy. He was so horny that it would only take two or three strokes and he would come, exploding with the desire he felt for Laura. He was suddenly dizzy and couldn't let go, either of his thoughts about Laura nor of his hard cock. He had to satisfy his lust.

But before he could begin to caress himself, the phone rang. Such an ordinary thing suddenly brought Anthony back to reality, and the guilt that followed was overwhelming.

*What the hell?* Anthony thought. *This girl is Philip's age!* How could he want a woman young enough be his daughter? In fact, she wasn't even a woman, but a girl. Anthony's feet seemed to be deep in the ground now, and the desire burning inside him seemed to be a little weaker.

✕

Hours went by, and Anthony was finally able to calm his nerves thanks to several shots of whiskey and *Led Zeppelin II* on the expensive stereo in his office. For the first time in many hours, time seemed to pass with a certain normality. Laura wouldn't show up again, nor would Anthony dare to step out of his office for a while. He waited until 7 o'clock that evening, by which time all his employees would be gone. He finally dared to leave his safe zone and found the whole office in a half-light. No one was there, he thought, but then there was Laura, standing at her desk. Anthony felt his heart pounding like never before; he felt terrified.

"She's just a girl..." he tried to convince himself, "Young enough to be your daughter."

Laura smiled and handed him a folder.

"Here, you forgot this, Mr. McReynolds."

Anthony walked slowly toward her and took the folder. For a moment, he felt safe. After all, he was a mature and experienced man. Laura, on the other hand, was just a young girl… what, nineteen? Twenty? Everything would be fine. No need to worry.

"Thank you very much, Miss Maeda. You've put in a good day's work, but it's time for you to get out of here and go home for today. If you don't get some sleep, you won't be able to focus on your classes tomorrow."

Laura laughed, making Anthony lose his hard-earned footing.

"Just what is it you're laughing at, Miss Maeda?"

"How do you see me, Mr. McReynolds?" asked Laura with unspeakable mischief in her eyes.

"I see you as a hard-working young girl."

Laura said nothing, but approached him with the most cynical smile Anthony had ever seen.

"I don't like it when you call me a *girl,* Anthony…"

*"Come and get it…"*

*"I must be out of my mind…"*

With that having been said, Laura opened her mouth. Slowly, rhythmically, her tongue slid out and licked her lips. At that moment, the mature and refined man regressed to a state of primitivism that even he himself was unaware of.

Anthony grabbed Laura in his arms with enough strength to break bones. Kissing her hard on the mouth, their tongues began to dance together. Laura began to suck on his tongue and then thrust her tongue into Anthony's mouth. How delicious her kisses were! Anthony's hands wasted no time caressing the small of her back, but went straight between her legs from behind. He discovered that Laura was dripping wet. Immediately Anthony's fingers slipped deep into her, in both orifices. She was moaning loudly, biting his lips to the point of making him bleed as his fingers delved deeper and deeper.

"Fuck me, please…" she said, nearly in tears.

Anthony grabbed Laura's tight little ass and set her on the desk, opening his pants and positioning himself between her legs, but upon seeing his hardness, she asked for more:

"Let me suck your cock first… I've wanted to do that ever since the first day we met."

Anthony nearly came just from hearing her say that. It had been so very long since the last time he felt desire like this, or felt that someone desired him. Laura knelt before him and nearly tore his trousers off, swirling her tongue over his heavy testicles and then swallowing his penis in a single motion.

Anthony nearly fainted. The feeling of that delicate, wet mouth on his penis… when was the last time he'd felt anything like that? Hard to say. Maybe never. So warm, so soft, so good…

He forgot his own age, or hers. He moaned loudly, grabbing Laura by her hair, and began to force his penis into her mouth even deeper.

"Yes… yes… fuck my mouth... cum inside my mouth," she begged, nearly gagging, those wicked eyes filled with tears. Saliva dripped from her mouth. Albert felt as if he was about to cum and tried to escape Laura's lips. He knew that once he came, it would be nearly impossible for him to get hard again. But when he tried to move, Laura grabbed his buttocks and pulled him into her mouth even harder. She did this three times before Anthony exploded. She tried to swallow it all, but it was too much too fast and in the end, Laura's face and breasts were covered in his semen.

Anthony felt out of breath, thoughts rushing through his mind. Philip, Julia, Laura, all swirled together in a shapeless mass. Feelings of guilt, sadness, deception. He looked down and saw the young woman he had defiled, and for a moment, Anthony felt as if he were the worst of all the low, horrible beings on the Earth.

Laura proceeded to remove the rest of her clothes and began to clean herself with some random article of clothing, making Anthony feel even more guilty.

"I'm sorry, I didn't…"

"Sorry for what?" said Laura, grabbing Anthony's cock and kissing him on the neck. It didn't take long for him to be hard again, much to his own delight. Without letting go of him, Laura sat on his desk and, spreading her legs as wide as a ballerina, said, "I'll only forgive you if you fuck my pussy as hard as you fucked my mouth."

Once again Anthony lost control of himself, and within a split second was inside Laura, thrusting deep into her, moaning and crying out. She rolled her hips and slapped his face.

"Just like this, you son of a bitch… tell me you always wanted to fuck me like this!"

Anthony was speechless.

"It's what you always wanted, isn't it?"

He groaned.

"Say it... say it, you bad, bad man!"

Anthony couldn't hold back any longer. Nothing at all, never again.

"Yes! Yes, it's what I always wanted...!"

"Always..." Laura had a look of suffering on her face, her eyes moist. It was as if she felt a very sharp pain, and was about to burst into tears at any moment. For a moment, it reminded Anthony of a painting he'd seen once, long ago, when Julia had dragged him to some art museum, somewhere, of the Virgin Mary standing at the foot of the Cross. Then it was gone, and there was only Laura. Wet, willing Laura.

"I've always wanted to fuck you, *so* hard..."

"Come... come with me... come inside me..."

Said and done. Both Anthony and Laura came at the same time; she cried and, amazingly, he ejaculated much more copiously than he had the first time. Then they slid gently across the table and fell exhausted onto the carpeted floor. Anthony was right; Laura cried during her orgasm.

✕

After that night there was no going back. Julia, at last, realized that something was very wrong. She went to Anna for advice and, as always, took Philip with her.

On the way, she told Philip, "Your father is cheating on me, Philip. I'm sure of it."

Philip, on the other hand, couldn't believe it. Anthony was rude, crude, nasty and fascist, but there's a limit to everything, and after all, Anthony was a man of honor, serious as only few men are. Philip told his inconsolable mother, "I'd put both my hands in the fire for him."

Things got even worse when Anthony began to spend nights at the office. Sometimes two, sometimes three, but usually only one night a week. "Too much work," he'd say, at that point no longer able to disguise his rising discomfort at home. Julia fell into despair, and from that point, Philip backed off from his willingness to stand up for his father.

✕

Around that time, Julia had gone to Anthony's office, something she had done only a few times before. She had felt no need to go there, not until this moment. As long as the cash kept coming in, Julia didn't get involved in Anthony's business.

As she entered the office, Julia was welcomed by Laura, who gave her an undisguisable cynical smile. *Fat old woman,* Laura thought, but she said, "Good morning, Mrs...?

"I'm Anthony's wife," said Julia, but she was thinking, *I'm your boss's wife, you Chinese whore!*

From their first look at each other, both women felt a sense of antagonism. Julia felt a vibe that told her that it was her, the Asian girl young enough to be her daughter. She was the reason why Anthony was feeling so uneasy at home, why he refused even the minimum of physical contact, why he would even spend nights at the office. Julia wanted to slap Laura in the face, once, twice. Ten times if necessary. She wanted to forget that she was a lady, embrace her wild side and show that stupid girl who was Anthony's woman.

But she didn't. Julia didn't know if it was out of her determination to remain a lady, or if she thought it would be best to avoid an assault charge, but in fact, the only thing Julia did was to repay cynicism with cynicism.

"What is your name?"

"My name is Laura Maeda."

"Very well, then, Miss Maeda; I need to ask you a favor."

Julia took a piece of paper from Laura's office stationery and wrote on it. "This is my phone number. If you notice anything odd, I want you to call me immediately."

"Odd?" smiled Laura. "Such as?"

*Oh, I don't know... like him losing the condom inside you... you fucking whore.*

"Like... you know, like him finding someone else."

"Having an affair?"

*Like you sucking my husband's dick until you gag... just exactly like that...*

"It's too early to say, but... yes, I would say so."

Laura was silent.

*Whores like you are like a swarm of grasshoppers…*

"You're quite young, but I'm sure you are fully aware that there are women out there with no problem having an affair with a married man."

"Yes, I know that…"

*As the saying goes, Bitches are bitches from the moment they find out there's a gap between their thighs…*

"Sadly, not only women, but even girls… young girls just like yourself."

Julia and Laura looked each other in the eye, blankly. Then Julia left without saying another word, feeling a turmoil of rage inside herself.

✕

Over time, the fighting between Anthony and Julia became more common and more vicious.

"Bastard! Just admit that you're having an affair with that little bitch!" Julia cried out, swinging at Anthony with the first object she saw that she thought would make a good weapon —a wooden clog that she had bought years before on a visit to Amsterdam. He managed to dodge two of the three blows, but the last one landed directly on its target. He didn't feel the impact, but it knocked him dizzy. His knees weakened and he had to lean against the wall to regain his footing. A trickle of rich blood began to flow from Anthony's forehead; his sight was so blurry that he couldn't tell Julia apart from Philip.

"Julia... what'd you do to me...?" said Anthony with a muffled voice.

The sight of blood seemingly aroused Julia even more, and she swung with even greater might, as if going for the killing blow.

"Damn you, you son of a..."

Rather than finish the sentence, Julia fell to the ground with a thud, feeling the right side of her face on fire.

Philip heard his mother's cry and ran into the room. Once there he saw Julia kneeling, her hand on the side of her face, while Anthony was standing there with an expression of pure horror on his face, shocked at what both he and Julia had done to each other.

"Philip... oh, Philip... come here to your mother," Julia groaned, tears rolling down over her face. Philip then ran toward his mother, never noticing the gash on his father's forehead. By the time Philip reached Julia, only the slamming of the front door could be heard. Anthony had left.

✕

"Laura?"

"Anthony...?"

"Can you meet me in an hour?"

"I'm a little busy with homework right now… college is boring stuff…"

*"Please…?"*

Laura heard the desperation in Anthony's voice, so unprotected and vulnerable. He clearly was in need of her, eager to be embraced and caressed. Laura couldn't resist.

"Okay, sure… where?"

✕

Laura and Anthony met on a quiet little street. He was the pure reflection of sadness, seemingly carrying the weight of the whole world on his shoulders. Blood still ran from the wound on his forehead. When Laura noticed the gash, she reached up to caress his slightly wrinkled face.

"Does it hurt very much?"

"There are worse ways of feeling pain, Laura… when you get old enough…"

Laura didn't say a word.

"I did something today I should never have done… something I never imagined that I would do."

Laura touched Anthony's face with both hands and looked him in the eye. She said, "Whatever you did, I know that you had your reasons." Bringing her lips toward his, she murmured, "Don't worry, I'll make you forget it all…"

As they made love, she thought of it as being like a magic trick; while he was inside her, thrusting himself back and forth until he exploded within her, there were no unsolved problems, no overwhelming guilt. It was just sheer, pure pleasure and joy.

Laura was distracted by Anthony's huge hands; his long fingers and his bulging knuckles. They were powerful hands, capable of gentle caresses yet able to grasp legs or buttocks firmly, the same type of strong hands that had saved her from the grasp of her horny teenaged boyfriend a few years back.

She remembered a cold December night several years before.

"I don't want it now," Laura had protested.

"Why *not?*" asked her angry boyfriend, whose name was Bobby. "You *always* say that —"

Laura was struggling in his grasp now.

"You get me all hot, all turned on, and then expect me to chill out in the blink of an eye, just like that..."

"I'm sorry... I'm just... I'm just not ready yet..."

"Are you fucking *kidding* me?"

"No... no, I'm not..."

"Do you realize how many times you've done this to me?"

"I —"

"You know what? Just get the fuck out. Get out of my car, you little ballbuster!"

Laura didn't move, but simply sat staring out of the windshield at the lights of the city far below. She knew Bobby had taken her to the middle of nowhere, and for him to expect her to walk home from here was laughable.

"How do you expect me to get home?" she asked.

"I don't give a *shit* how you get home! Hitch a ride with another couple after they're finished doing it! Now fuck off!"

He got out of the driver's side and circled around to Laura's door. He threw the passenger door open, and dragged her out into the frosty night air, smacking and punching her as he did so. There were eight or ten other vehicles parked nearby, all there for the same thing Bobby had wanted, all ignoring what was happening to her.

All at once she was free of his grasp, kneeling on the dirt next to the car. Confused, she looked up to see a strange man dragging her abuser away, toward the back of the car; she couldn't see his face, but what she did see was one massive hand grasping the shoulder of Bobby's faded denim jacket. It dwarfed Bobby's abusive hands, which were flailing around trying to break free, to no avail.

"Lemme *go!* Get your hands —" Bobby was yelling.

To no avail. Suddenly Laura's mysterious savior spun Bobby around so that they were face to face. She heard him say, "You oughta learn to treat ladies better." There was a *THWOP* sound — she swore it was like the sound you would imagine from a blow struck in a comic book — and Bobby fell to the ground like a hundred-pound sack of feed, or what Laura *imagined* a hundred-pound sack of feed would sound like as it fell to the ground, at least; she had never even been on a farm.

"Can I give you a ride home?" said her savior, his face still shadowed.

"I, uh… okay," she said.

"I'm parked over here," he said, his voice low and rumbly, and crossed over to the other side of the clearing. He had a late 60s or early 70s model Buick, one of the big boats… it was gold with a white vinyl top. To Laura, it looked like an angelic chariot.

The big man — and he *was* big, Laura didn't even stand as high as his shoulder, and she wasn't that short at 5'8" — came around and opened her door for her. She climbed in to the passenger side; white leather interior, and it was nice and warm inside; he'd left it running.

He climbed into the driver's side and she saw his face in the dim light. She didn't know him; his crystal blue eyes twinkled at her in the dim light. He was nicely dressed, in a suit and tie. What he had been doing out here on Lookout Hill, she had no idea.

"Who *are* you?" she asked.

"Just somebody who saw something bad happening and needed to stop it."

He put the car in gear and they drove down from the hilltop. He didn't ask directions. He seemed to know where to go. Soon they were in front of Laura's parents' house.

"What's your name?" she blurted out.

"It doesn't matter," said the man.

"It does to *me!*"

"You can call me Gabe."

She got out and watched him drive away and then walked toward the house. Tiny blue lights lined the roof.

✕

Ever since that night, Laura had had a 'thing' for older men, strong men who had a sense of style and decorum. What she hadn't been able to accomplish with Gabe — stripping away his cool detachment as well as his clothing, and giving him what she believed every man wanted — she accomplished with a string of men, up and down the Eastern seaboard.

✕

Anthony's hands reminded Laura of those strong hands, but he was certainly no avenging angel. A *fallen* one, maybe.

She stood on her tiptoes and kissed him hard.

# 17: THE SEPARATION

It had been a beautiful morning, probably the sunniest of the whole year, when Anthony returned home. He had just spent yet another night away from home, and now, as he walked into the house, he brought the scent of Laura with him, all over his skin.

He tried to be as silent as possible, but it didn't work. Julia had spent the night awake, just as he had, but rather than the cause being pleasure and lust, it was despair and sadness that kept her from sleep. Philip had spent the night awake as well, washing his mother's tears. He reassured her that everything would be all right, though all the while he never believed it.

There was Anthony, standing in front of his family, wishing he could melt away like vapor. The payback for his pleasure was now unbearable shame. He didn't say a word; he knew it would be useless. He simply sat down on the couch and stayed there, breathing hard, as if he was choking.

*The bastard is waiting for the first opportunity to get out,* thought Philip. he couldn't forgive his father for having slapped his mother in the face. Still, he didn't say a word. The entire house was engulfed by dead silence.

Anthony wanted to walk out through the door, never to return, but after a few seconds of imagining his departure, he couldn't stand the thought of leaving his family behind. Anthony wouldn't make a move. Julia finally came to him. If not for the tears, her red eyes would have looked like those of a doll.

"You don't want to be here anymore…"

Anthony said nothing, but simply looked at the floor.

"So you can leave... no need to stay in here out of pity or guilt… just leave. Just…"

Julia couldn't say another word, but burst into tears. Philip was by his mother's side, holding her tightly.

"Julia… I…" said Anthony, trying to touch her face, but he was suddenly interrupted by Philip.

"Just leave, Dad. Please, just go."

✕

Anthony didn't pack. He went out the same way he had come in. Now, driving his car, headed to only God knew where, dissolving into tears and grief, he was engulfed by memories of all the good times he'd had with Julia.

✕

Julia, who had been so strong by letting her unfaithful husband go, lost all her strength after that day and became slightly obsessed. Even though it was clear that there was no hope of rebuilding her shattered marriage, Julia retreated into a world of her own in which everything that happened was just a crisis.

In order to feed this illusion, she needed to blame someone else for Anthony's behavior. First it was herself, and then Philip became the responsible party. She shouted at him, over and over, bursting into tears again and again:

*You've ruined my marriage!*

*I hate you! I should have given you to the orphanage! At least I'd still have my husband by my side right now!*

Many times Philip said nothing; not because he didn't feel offended, but because he had let go of any hope of making his mother see reality. Julia had never been, even on her best days, a person who would willfully engage in any conversation in which she could not be the victim, or the standard of perfection. Now that Julia had framed Philip as the architect of her misfortune, there was no hope. Neither God nor the Devil would be able to dissuade her from that idea.

It was a difficult time. Philip preferred to be away from home. Then he took a job at the first opening he found and felt grateful every day for not having to see his mother so often.

✕

Another day dawned, dismal and grey. After leaving Arthur's office and arriving home, Philip noticed that Julia wasn't there. It was a bittersweet relief; having his mother away from home for a few hours would make him feel much better. He usually felt guilty about everything, but this time was different: Aunt Anna had successfully convinced Julia to accept the services of the lawyer she'd enlisted. From that day on, the two ladies spent their afternoons and evenings at coffee shops and restaurants, discussing the best way to dig as deeply as possible into Anthony's pockets.

Peace, at last. For how long? It was hard to say, but now Philip would have time to enjoy his recently discovered hobby, admiring a picture he had printed from Amanda's profile.

"She's so pretty..." sighed Philip.

*Amanda...* "Worthy to be loved…"

Philip also remembered the things she had written on her profile:

*... I like to sleep listening to the rain falling on the roof...*

He felt so strange while imagining what she must be like. He was afraid, and at the same time, excited. By the time he gathered the courage to make the call, his heart was pounding. Philip dialed the number carefully, paying attention to the piece of paper where he'd written down Amanda's phone number.

The phone rang once... twice... three times, and still no answer. Philip hung up, having read on one of the sites that some girls might think that a guy who let the phone ring more than three times was a creep or a stalker. Philip was now in a dead end situation. He was really interested in contacting Amanda, but insistence might have the opposite effect. So what to do?

He called again a bit later, and wondered if she had an answering device of any kind. Just as he was thinking about this, he was surprised by a beep and a recorded message.

"Hi there! This is Amanda. Leave your name and number and I'll call you back... bye!"

Her voice was so soft, it sounded like a pack of mermaids singing along. Philip shivered. It would be ridiculous to think he was falling in love just from her voice on the phone... and still, he had a strange feeling about her.

×

"I know it's hard for you to believe, but there are other ways to find a girlfriend... you know, like *face to face...*?" grinned Henry. "You have to get close, face to face, eye to eye. And quit wasting time with those skanks from the dating sites. Most of those girls are ugly as sin, when you get lucky enough to find an actual girl... if you know what I mean."

Philip felt uneasy on that occasion. Now, after listening to Amanda's recording, he thought that maybe it really was a good idea to try to deal more in the realms of reality. Maybe it was time to step back and quit Internet dating.

But there was something so irresistible about Amanda. It was hard to say if it was her pixie haircut, her sad eyes or the phrase, "I like to sleep listening to the rain falling on the roof." How many souls in this world besides Amanda and Philip appreciated the rain?

"Whatever!" thought Philip. That would be his last attempt. If things went down with her like it had with Maurina, he'd be done with Internet dating once and for all. He left her a message:

"Hi, Amanda. My name is Philip... I got your phone number from a dating website. I really liked your profile. Not many people around who like the rain, you know… well, if you have the time and are interested, give me a call back. Cheers."

And since he knew it was the last time he'd make a call like this, Philip let some of his dissatisfaction slip out with a slightly acid joke: "I gotta ask, but... is this some kind of prank?"

After he hung up, Philip felt a little regret for asking that, but in any case there was no way to take it all too seriously. The odds were all against it, anyway. Amanda lived in another city and a long distance relationship was bound to be a lot of trouble.

# 18: AMANDA

Two days had passed, and Amanda had not contacted Philip. He went on with his dating routine and ran across a girl who wanted to arouse jealousy in her ex-boyfriend. It worked well, and Philip was nearly punched in the face by the ex as well as a group of his friends. Still, the girl couldn't get her relationship back in order. She decided she wanted to keep seeing Philip and kept on calling him.

He quickly crossed her off his list. At least he'd gotten to kiss Maurina. With this new girl, he'd nearly ended up kissing her jealous boyfriend's fist.

*"Next time I see you, I'm gonna kick your ass, punk!"*

From then on, every time the girl called, Philip would do his elderly French gentleman's imitation. So far it had been working very well.

"Hello, I want to talk to Philip."

*"Pardonnez-moi... Je ne comprends pas..."*

"What?"

*"J'ai dit... Je ne comprends pas."*

"Are you a *Mexican...?"*

After saying that, the girl usually hung up. She had little patience with those unable to speak her language. In fact, the nameless girl seemed to believe that even in China the official language was English.

Philip was getting tired of this situation, despite it being a little amusing to make fun of her. One day, when the phone rang unexpectedly, he would pick it up, already getting into the French mood. But then...

*"Oui...?"*

"Hello... I would like to talk to Philip," said an unfamiliar voice. Not just a voice, but pure melody. For sure it wasn't the nameless girl. It had to be....

"I'm Philip... And you are...?"

"Wow... for a second I thought I'd dialed the wrong number," the voice said, with a tone of amusement. "Oh, I'm sorry, I'm Amanda."

"Amanda..." Philip repeated her name, hypnotized by the sound of her voice. He never heard a voice like that before. So smooth, still so vivacious.

"Don't you know who I am?"

"Sure! Sure! Amanda. Of course I know who you are... I gave you a call three days ago..."

"Two," she said. Philip could hear her smiling.

"Yes, two... time goes fast sometimes."

"See, it wasn't a prank." Again the smile.

"I'm glad it wasn't. Wow, it's funny hearing your voice on the phone…"

"Funny as in goofy?"

"No, no! Far from it… just kinda… *different.* So far I've only seen your pictures, and now you have a voice"

"Kind of… step by step, becoming more… more…"

"Real?"

"Yes… you know, I thought the same thing when I heard your message on my phone, the one about the prank… I replayed it a few times. It felt different… you sorta stepped out from the Internet straight into the real world."

"I feel the same way."

"Did you like my voice?"

"Yeah, I did… it's beautiful."

"Liar…" This time Philip didn't have to picture her smile; Amanda laughed softly."

"Amanda… can I ask you something?"

"Sure."

"Do you really like the rain?"

"Yes. I like it a lot. Here in Buffalo it rains a lot. I'm kinda out of options. Either I like it, or I'll have to pack up and leave."

"Well…"

"But I feel peaceful anyplace where it rains…" This brought a smile to Philip's lips.

The phone call didn't take long, about twenty minutes or so, as Amanda had some errands to take care of, but it felt in some ways like a mere twenty seconds and in others like twenty hours. Philip promised he would return the call the next evening.

*Daily Journal: Hello...*

*Today I confirmed what I had already suspected: my mother does not want me to be happy. I met someone so special, so sensitive and so passionate... So there was no way, I think I ended up falling in love... and do you know what my mother did? She said I should worry more about my studies...*

*Do all mothers behave like this?*

*Kasumi*

# 19: SPARKS

Philip got a haircut, and then went shopping. He bought a travel bag and a set of new clothes: a tee-shirt topped with a flannel shirt, both in dark colors. It was a cold Saturday morning, and Julia's words still echoed in his head:

"How *dare* you, boy?! Show some respect for your mother, you *brat!*" shouted Julia. An argument had begun, seemingly over nothing. The real reason, however, was Philip's planned trip to Buffalo.

"How can you leave me alone for an entire weekend? Especially right now, when I'm facing a court battle with your father?"

Philip looked at the floor, willing himself not to lash out at her.

"Philip…"

"Look, Mom, I'm sorry, but I already asked Henry to let me borrow his car," Philip argued.

"So you're planning to drive six hours to meet a girl that you know nothing about?"

"Mom —"

"You can find lots of girls just as good as her here, close to home… but you only have *one* mother…"

*I'd be better off having none,* Philip thought. He immediately felt guilty. Still, he said nothing.

"Talk to me, Philip. Are you really going to insist on your little road trip, all the way to Buffalo?"

"Mom," he said with a defeated tone in his voice.

"So you're not going. I'll call Henry for you and tell him you've decided not to go... besides, how in the world would Anna have allowed him to lend you his car? Is everybody around me just losing their minds?"

*Of course we are... and you started it all. Madness is a disease that's spreading and you are its source, mother...*

"So you want me to call him for you, right?"

"Mom... actually, I don't..."

Julia gave him a look that could have killed.

"I really want to go..."

Julia was silent.

Philip was silent as well.

"I'll call Anna in the morning, then."

Philip suddenly mustered the courage to do something he'd never dared to do before. He actually refused a request from his mother.

"Mom, I do *not* want you to call Henry... and by the way, Anna doesn't have a damned thing to do with it. It's *Henry's* car; *he's* letting me borrow it, and I am *going* to Buffalo."

Julia looked at Philip with a sick look in her eyes. She looked as if she were about to burst into tears. When Philip didn't show any signs of relenting, her face fell. She looked as though she had been stabbed in the back.

"Oh, my son... my son... you're going to leave your old mother...?"

"Jesus Christ, Mother. You're acting like I'm moving to Tibet! I'll only be gone for *two days*. You'll survive!"

Julia said nothing, but retreated to her bedroom sanctuary and the sweet embrace of more Valium.

From that moment on, Philip tried to keep his focus away from Julia's diatribe. He knew the meds would soon carry her off to dreamland.

✕

*"Mr. Keller...?" Philip said, rapping gently on Arthur's office door.*

*"Yes, Philip...? What can I do for you?"*

*"Well... there's something I need to ask you..."*

As he drove up Interstate 80, Philip thought of the appalled expression that had crossed Arthur's face. The man looked as if he had been just hit by lightning. It was sort of fun seeing him like this; the man was normally so in control of everything that went on in the office. Philip could tell that his double request for a payroll advance and the following Friday off was something that stuck in his craw, but he really had no valid reason to refuse him. Philip then began to laugh to himself, until a careless truck driver whose rig was drifting slightly into his land brought him back to the real world.

The conversation he'd had with Henry also amused him:

"Come on, now, buddy… you promise you're gonna take good care of my pretty baby, right…?"

"Henry… how long have we been friends…?"

"A lifetime… literally."

"So doesn't that mean anything to you?"

"If it didn't, we wouldn't even be having this conversation."

"So?"

"It's been ages since the last time you drove a car…"

"Don't be so dramatic. I'll take care just as if it was my own."

"That's just what I'm afraid of." The look in Henry's eyes would have been priceless if he'd been playing a prank on him. At the time it had been annoying, but now, driving Henry's classic Citroën convertible north toward Binghamton, Philip simply smiled. Henry might as well have been his brother. He knew how much this trip meant to Philip, and would never have said no to him, but he did love his car.

From Binghamton, Philip would make his way westward to Buffalo, where he would meet the woman that he was sure would change his life forever.

Philip hadn't said goodbye to his mother; she was out like a light anyway. He left her a note on the dining room table and left. Henry had been waiting for him on the street and asked him one more time to take good care of his car. Then he caught a cab to get to work.

Philip waited until Henry had gone to start the Citroën's engine. Henry was right; it had been ages since the last time he drove, but it was fine. Amanda was worthy of any sacrifice.

✕

For the first several weeks after their first contact through the dating site, Amanda and Philip's relationship had slowly begun to grow. However, in Philip's eyes it was moving much too slowly; Amanda was still taking it very carefully. Although they had much in common and felt strongly attracted to each other, Amanda was unwilling to allow herself to commit too strongly as long as they had not met in person; she was of the opinion that until that happened, they should consider themselves just friends; two people sharing similar tastes and interests, but that was all. This was something that frustrated Philip immensely.

"Oh, my angel," she said as they talked on the phone late into the night, "I like you so much... very, *very* much... but I think it's too early to be sure about so many of the things you're talking about..."

"I don't need to see you in person to know that what I feel is real," Philip replied impatiently.

"I feel something, too, sweetheart, but even you can't be sure of how you feel… you've never actually *met* me…"

"I *love* you, Amanda…" She was silent as he continued. "I think about you all the time…"

"So do I!"

"Isn't this love?"

"Philip… I don't know yet."

Philip felt mortally wounded by her words. There he was, engulfed by the intensity of his feelings, and Amanda kept pushing him away. Still more painful was the fact that Philip could understand why, even if he didn't agree. How could Amanda love him if they had never met in person? How could they be sure about being in love? As Amanda said, not even Philip himself could be sure about his feelings.

Still, Philip hadn't been completely rational at that point. He was desperately in need of love. He needed to love and to be loved. He needed to hear '*I love you*' more than his lungs needed oxygen.

Amanda was as excited as Philip, but she knew they were both too lonely and needy to understand clearly what was going on in their hearts. Amanda realized, too, that Philip didn't necessarily have this same insight.

"We agree on everything. Why on earth, then, can she not like me? *Love* me?" Philip still had in mind the "chemistry lecture" he'd been given by Maurina.

Despite that, and despite his feelings of having been wronged, he decided to take a leap of faith and risk it all.

He went to Badi's shop and began to write a farewell e-mail to Amanda.

Amanda

Well, I`ve spent time thinking about what we talked about, and I think you`re right. Maybe we`ve been rushing things. Maybe when we know each other better

*No, not like this,* He thought, I've got nothing to lose. There's no point of being afraid of losing something I never had. He discarded what he'd typed, and began a new message:

Amanda, I think this message will be my last. I`m a little tired of being rejected. If you felt the way I feel, you would have no doubts... And if you don`t feel the same, I think there`s no point in continuing with this. We`re all blind to the things we don`t want to see, as well as deaf to the things we don`t want to hear... I am no exception.

Philip

Philip felt like plunging a dagger into his own heart as he clicked Send. As he headed back home, a teardrop rolled down his cheek.

The next day, when he stopped at Badi's, Philip had two email messages, something that rarely occurred. They were both from Amanda. As he got ready to open them, he thought that she probably was going to tell him to go to hell. Philip had no small amount of regret for sending the e-mail the day before.

*I pushed her too far. I shouldn't have done that,* thought Philip. Where would such a stupid idea have come from? From his troubled mind. Why the hell did you decided to make an ultimatum to Amanda? Now it was already too late. Certainly she had written him back in order to finish off what he, in his endless stupidity, had begun.

"Okay," Philip muttered. He was already sick of these fruitless "social networking sites" and the fruitless dates he garnered from them. Besides, Amanda was living in another city, four hundred miles away — six hours by car. No way. It would never work. It *could* never work.

He began to hear a plaintive song in his head as he began to open his e-mail. The first one was more or less what Philip was expecting:

```
Philip

I don`t get what just happened. I really
don`t. We were doing well, and suddenly, out of
nowhere you wrote me those things. It made me
feel bad when I read it. Really. You made me
cry, you know...

I`m sorry for being kind of restrained, but
my parents don`t give me that much alone time,
not even in my room, and it would freak my mom
out to suddenly hear me saying I love you to
somebody.
```

**Bye...**

**Amanda**

The first thought that occurred to Philip was to immediately call Amanda and apologize for everything he'd said, perhaps even telling Amanda how stressful his daily life was, and how much stress Julia put on Philip... Amanda would likely understand that things were partly motivated by the unbearable emotional distress to which he was exposed every day.

*Would Amanda understand all this?*

*Of course she would... Amanda was not only beautiful, but also delicate and wise.*

Yes... this is how it should be. It was the best or perhaps the only option. if Amanda didn't know how bad his life was, Philip would seem like a crazy man, nothing but some random nutjob. He was ready to open up to her: no more secrets. She would have to know everything. After he read the second message from Amanda, he'd e-mail her back and open himself to her. But then...

**My angel**

I`m sorry I`m such a fool. Forgive me for so often not knowing what to say... I`m also beginning to love you, but I`m just so scared to admit it. I was afraid, because I suddenly realized that you do not necessarily feel the way you think you do... I know it sounds silly, but what if you don`t feel the same way when we meet in person? I would be left with a broken heart. Anyway... I think I`m just a fool terrified of everything.

I hope you`re not angry with me anymore, little angel... Well, I`ll be at home tonight at 9:00 p.m. If you want to give me a call, I would love it. In fact, I want you to call... I`ll be waiting for you...

I do love you... please don`t be upset with me...

Amanda

The smile on Philip's lips was so wide that anyone who saw it would have thought he must have won the lottery. Philip felt something that he had never felt before: pure happiness.

"She loves me... she *loves* me!"

Philip kept repeating it to himself. He just could not believe it.

As if he were walking over the clouds, Philip returned home, feeling even more blessed by the absence of his mother. He spent the hours counting down to the moment when he could finally call Amanda, an eternity that, in the end, didn't take so long: after three long rings, Amanda answered.

"Hello," said Amanda, as always, a little shy.

"Hi..." Philip answered, without knowing for sure what to say.

She remained silent for a few seconds; this time however, it was impossible for Philip to wait.

"Amanda... did you really cry?"

"I... I did... I felt horrible..."

Upon hearing that, Philip felt like he'd been stabbed. As he imagined the tears coming from her beautiful eyes, covering the soft skin of her face, h almost cried himself.

"Amanda... I'm sorry... I'm *so* sorry... I... I was confused, and scared..."

"It's all right, I understand."

"I'm sorry... Please forgive me...?"

"It's okay, really... I understand you. I really do."

"So you're not upset with me?"

"How could I be...? I love you!"

Philip's heart began pounding as he heard those words. He tried to say once again that he loved her but he could not; the emotions running furiously through him wouldn't allow it. As Amanda went on, Philip became even more speechless.

"It doesn't matter what you do to me. I feel like I can't be angry at you... I love you! You're my angel."

When he heard those words, Philip found his voice once again.

"I love you, too... I loved you from the very first time I saw your picture, from the first moment I heard your voice... I'm so sorry, Amanda. I didn't mean to make you cry..."

"I think I kind of deserved it… you know, I kinda needed a wake-up call. I needed you to wake me up from being closed in."

"Still, it didn't have to be like this," Philip said sorrowfully.

"I don't think there was any other way… I was afraid, so afraid of you… and more than anything, I was afraid of myself. I've never told you this, but I dreamt about you…"

"I dream of you, too... sometimes even while I'm wide awake…"

"You just made me so confused... before you came along, I always knew when I met someone whether I liked them as a friend, or if… you know… if it was something more than that. With you, it was totally different. I think it was because I was never really in love before. If it wasn't for your message, it would have taken longer for me to realize what was going on with me…"

"I would have waited as long as I had to."

Amanda laughed a little, sounding so happy. "You shouldn't say that, dear heart. You almost let me go."

"I'm so sorry… I wrote that, but I wouldn't have done it… I couldn't have." Philip felt a twinge of guilt. There was no need to have made her cry. It would have been enough to have had her friendship. He should have been a little more patient, given her enough time. "I love you," he said.

"I love you, too... you're my angel. I love you so much…" she paused thoughtfully. Each of them was still learning the joy of hearing the other utter declarations of love, something that neither of them had ever experienced before.

"My angel..." said Amanda.

"Yes...?" smiled Philip.

"So now, we're... like... boyfriend and girlfriend?" For weeks, since first getting Philip's initial inquiry online, Amanda had longed for the time when she would no longer feel alone. Now, finally, the moment had arrived.

"Yes, my love," said Philip. "Yes, we are... a couple."

"So say it."

"Say what...?"

"Say I'm your girlfriend, and you're my boyfriend."

Philip smiled. "You're my girlfriend and I'm your boyfriend."

✕

*If this is a dream, I never want to wake up...*

# 20: SHUFFLE OFF

After six long, frustrating hours, Philip finally reached the outskirts of Buffalo, near West Seneca. The rain was coming down heavily and it was a little colder than he had expected. He got off I-90 at the Ridge Road exit and went east to Orchard Park Road, following the directions that Amanda had given him. Then he stopped in the parking lot at K-Mart.

Philip noticed that Henry had left a jacket in the back seat of the car. He slipped it on, then took out his cell phone. Amanda had told him *As soon as you get to Buffalo, give me a call.* Amanda's voice echoing in Philip's head was the sweetest thing he'd ever heard, and he kept mentally replaying it while dialing her number. Then, as always, after the third ring, Amanda answered.

"Hello?"

"Hi, Amanda. I'm in West Seneca, like you said."

"Oh, really? Wow, that was fast. Where are you?" she asked. He'd never heard Amanda sound so excited. There were two other voices in the background; a middle-aged male and an older woman, probably Amanda's mother.

"I'm sitting in the parking lot in front of the K-Mart on Orchard Park Road."

"We'll be there in a bit."

✕

It didn't take very long, and yet to Philip, the time was counted in heartbeats rather than minutes. Then his phone rang.

"Hi, Philip... um... we're here in front of Tim Horton's. Dad wanted to get a coffee," said Amanda, sounding more anxious than ever. Her words were interspersed by nervous giggles and the voice of her mother. "We're in a silver Toyota Highlander."

"I think I can see you from here. I'm coming to you. I'm in a blue Citroën, and I'm wearing a black jacket," said Philip. He thought for a moment that he came off too cool. *Maybe this jacket and this car are affecting my attitude,* he thought. A black jacket and a black shirt... maybe it was too dark after all. But in any case, Philip hadn't come for a funeral. He was about to meet the girl of his dreams. He'd finally be able to see her, touch her, smell her perfume, maybe even kiss her. As these thoughts began to flow through his mind, a bright and possibly slightly goofy smile formed on his face. By the time he pulled up next to Amanda and her parents, his smile could have lit up the darkest night.

✕

By the time his car was within about fifty yards from her, Amanda could see Philip clearly. She felt her heart tighten, her hands began to shake and she discovered a new sign of anxiety: her lips went numb and cold.

*He's so handsome... what if he doesn't like me? This shirt is weird looking. It doesn't go with my jacket... My makeup is too heavy... no, it's too light... I look like someone who just got out of bed...*

Amanda bit her lower lip slightly, a nervous habit. Philip smiled when he saw that. She was so sexy, and she wasn't even aware of it. Or maybe that's *why* she was so sexy... her awkward innocence.

✕

When he parked next to them, and even more clearly as he got out of the Citroën and walked around toward their car, Philip could see Amanda and a middle-aged couple by her side. He knew these had to be her parents, even though neither of them looked anything like Amanda.

Amanda herself was a little different than how Philip imagined, or how the pictures she sent had revealed. She wore a slightly extravagant floral blouse under a hot pink jacket. She was a little shorter than he'd pictured, her hair a little longer, slightly wavier than any of her photos, and also a little lighter. In person her slightly Asian appearance was more prominent. Her delicate features made her look a little like a porcelain doll.

In truth, he had never given much thought to what her parents might be like. For that matter, he had never really thought about them at all.

Her father was an interesting type. Surprisingly short. Gray, spiky hair, well dressed. Amanda's mother was in a league of her own. Her face, her height and everything else about her seemed very average, but there was something wicked about her, something difficult to understand. Philip just got a negative feeling from her.

"You must be Philip, I'm Paul, Amanda's dad. It's very nice to meet you," said the spiky-haired man as he stretched out his hand with a smile.

"Nice to meet you, Mr. Robinson," Philip said, shaking the man's hand. Despite his short stature, he had a robust physique and, perhaps on purpose, almost crushed Philip's fingers with his grip. It seemed to be an unspoken message: *Just a warning of what can happen to you if you ever hurt my baby girl...*

"Hello, Philip, I'm Suzan," said Amanda's mother, shaking his hand with far less strength. She was a tall woman with wavy, flaming red hair.

Then Amanda stepped forward with an adorable, shy look on her face to greet Philip.

They embraced briefly; Philip started to give her a quick kiss on the cheek, but she drew back self-consciously. He realized that Amanda was probably hesitant to let him kiss her in front of her parents. Her perfume was sweet, even sweeter than Emma's. Philip blinked and lingered for a second. By keeping his eyes closed he felt like Amanda was an angel, there to escort him to Paradise.

"My car is over there," said Philip, still in a daze.

Mr. Robinson's voice broke through his reverie, saying, "Yes, son, we saw you pull up... and you're parked right next to us," he said, smiling.

"Oh… yes, sir."

"Earth to Philip," laughed Suzan slightly. "So, tell us about yourself."

"Well, I'm nineteen years old…"

"Are you attending college?"

"Not yet. I'm working in a real estate office."

"Selling houses?"

"No… just as a gofer, at this point."

"Next year, Mandy is planning to go to the University of Rochester. She wants to get her degree in Art."

"I think that suits her very well," Philip said.

"Sure it does. My little Mandy is a gifted artist," said Suzan, pinching Amanda's cheek as if she were three years old. Amanda rolled her eyes.

"Mom…" protested Amanda, clearly embarrassed.

"Don't worry, Mandy, I'm sure Philip understands the love a mother has for her child," smiled Suzan. Staring at Philip, she continued: "You have a mother, don't you, Philip?"

*Sure, she's just as twisted as you are…*

"Yes, ma'am."

Paul was the one who came to Philip's rescue.

"You must be tired, Philip, but we'd like you to have lunch with us and then, I guess, Mandy has some plans of her own. So what if you come ride with us, and tomorrow we'll see about whether you and Mandy can go places in your car? What do you say?"

Philip felt a mixed sense of relief. It was true that he was tired. He'd been driving for six straight hours, and was ready for some rest and time off from being behind the wheel. But on the other hand, he had been looking forward to being alone with Amanda.

"Sure, whatever you like, Mr. Robinson."

"And Philip…"

"Yessir?"

"Please, just call me Paul."

*A friendly middle-aged man… why can't my father be like this?*

✕

Philip climbed into the back seat of the Robinson's silver Toyota SUV. Amanda's family got in, Paul started the car and they took off. Judging by the way Paul drove, Philip quickly understood that the car was a source of pride to him. It still smelled new.

They headed northward on Orchard Park Road, which soon turned into Potters Road, and then into Abbott Road. They passed through an area with some beautiful older homes, several of which had large white columns in the front. They reminded Philip of his parents' old home, which he missed. He saw a shop with Irish flags hanging on the front, and later two or three sweet shoppes nearby each other on the right, followed by a dental office on the left; the irony made Philip smile a bit.

He tried to pay attention to landmarks, hoping he could find his way back to Henry's car in case they decided to leave him somewhere. In his nervousness, Philip imagined them deciding he wasn't good enough for Amanda and leaving him stranded miles from the car. His stomach began to churn from the long journey, and he hoped he wasn't going to be sick right there in the back of the Robinson's car, next to Amanda. He hoped it wouldn't be much further to wherever they were going.

During the trip, only Suzan spoke, and that almost compulsively: "So what do you think of Buffalo? Do you like it?"

*Having been here less than twenty minutes, I would say it's a little early to have an opinion,* Philip thought. What he said was, "It's very nice."

That phrase was the only one Philip could come up with. Suzan kept pointing to sights and asking him whether he liked them. Often he didn't understand what Suzan was talking about until it was too late to see anything. He kept smiling, playing along and hoping that Suzan would calm down. Sadly, this never seemed to happen.

The road turned slightly to the left and became South Park Avenue. They continued driving; Philip began to wonder if they would ever stop.

And then, with his ears nearly numb, he heard the sweet voice of Amanda. "Philip…" she said in a low murmur.

"Yes…?"

"You see that place, the one with the cherry blossom trees?"

"Yes, they're beautiful…"

"They really are. That's one of my very favorite places. Sometimes, in the springtime, I come over here to draw. They're not big deal right now, but you should see them in the spring."

"They're really beautiful. The cherry trees, I mean." After saying that, Philip looked at Amanda. He noticed that she kept her head a little low, staring at the floor, displaying a certain sadness mingled with insecurity. At that moment, Philip felt so much affection for her. He felt the need to embrace her and caress her hair. Philip needed to whisper in her ear, *"Everything will be okay…"*

Philip looked into Amanda's eyes, and said with a smile, "You're every bit as beautiful as the cherry trees."

Amanda blushed instantly and Suzan didn't miss the opportunity for a joke: "I bet you get all the ladies, don't you, Philip…?"

"Oh, no, Mrs. Robinson, far from it…"

Amanda stayed silent until they reached the Walden Galleria.

✕

They took Amanda and Philip into the mall. Philip didn't pay too much attention to the place. He kept thinking, *I can't wait to be alone with her.*

Having Amanda by his side made the long trip worth it. They walked through the stores hand in hand, just a few steps behind Paul and Suzan, who continued to glance back at them over their shoulders.

"From here, we're going to the pet shop." Suzan said, "and then we'll get some lunch."

"That'll be great," Philip said.

"By the way, did you call your mother?" asked Suzan.

"No, not yet…" Philip said.

"You should take the time to do that," she said. "Mothers always worry about their children."

*Oh, sure, calling her would be a great idea,* he thought. No doubt she'd complain for at least an hour. Philip knew that problems would start as soon as he dialed her number, so he decided to put it off until later.

"I'll call her when I get to my hotel room, Mrs. Robinson."

"All right, Philip. You know best."

✕

They went to a pet shop because Paul and Suzan wanted to look at birds. Paul was an avid bird enthusiast. *Look at your wife,* Philip thought, looking at Suzan's brilliant red curls. *She looks like a parrot.* Maybe that was why she and Paul got along.

They spent so long in the pet store that Philip's stomach begin to growl with hunger. Finally, the Robinsons were ready to go to lunch.

×

They finally settled on a place to eat. "I'm craving a bacon cheeseburger," said Paul. "I'm absolutely starving!"

They sat down and began to look over the menu. Amanda decided on Chicken Almondine; Suzan ordered a salad and pineapple juice. Paul laughed and ordered the bacon cheeseburger that he had wanted, and encouraged Philip to have the same.

After everyone had placed their orders, they sat in an uncomfortable silence for a few moments.

Suzan kept staring at him, as if she were scanning him for some flaw, something that she could use against him in the future if it became necessary.

"So, Philip..." said Suzan as she settled into her chair at the restaurant, "Since you aren't going to school, what do you do?"

"I work…"

"What sort of job do you have?"

"I work at a real estate office," Philip responded. He recalled telling them this when they had first met, but said nothing.

"Oh, yes, that's right. As a gofer. Well, don't get me wrong, but…" She coughed softly. "It sounds a little like a… how can I say this politely? Frankly, it sounds like a dead end job."

"Mom!" said Amanda.

Suzan smiled and said, "I'm just being sincere. I think you should always be straightforward, don't you, Philip?"

*Sincerity might be like curiosity and you might be the cat,* thought Philip. He said nothing, but merely smiled. It was becoming clear to him that Suzan and Julia had a lot in common.

Paul felt the uneasiness and changed the subject.

"So, Philip — who do you like in the playoffs?"

✕

After finishing their lunch, Paul insisted that Suzan accompany him as he went to get fitted for a new suit at his favorite tailor shop while Philip and Amanda be allowed to roam the mall to their heart's content.

As they parted, Suzan stared at him for a moment and said, "Philip, you have such sad eyes."

# 21: FINALLY PASAGARDA

Amanda and Philip were now finally alone. Now, after so much time wishing and waiting, there was nothing and no one between them.

Philip kept some distance between them as they walked, and that made her feel rather insecure. Judging by Philip's posture, she felt like he had been disappointed in her, somehow, when they met in person.

"You can come a little closer... if you want to," said Amanda as they went up the escalator to the top floor, mistaking Philip's shyness for a lack of interest in her.

Philip smiled and gently touched the tip of Amanda's nose. There was a small birthmark there, just a spot, almost like a freckle. Amanda whispered, "I'm so glad you're finally here..."

Philip leaned in and pressed his cheek against hers, their first real physical contact. He put his arms around her, breathing in her delicate perfume. Philip smiled and Amanda gave him a brief kiss on the lips.

She was so sweet, so tender... Philip couldn't remember when he had been treated with so much love.

"Can I have another one?" he asked.

"Soon, but not here, my angel," smiled Amanda.

It was the first time she had called him her angel in person. The cool demeanor that Philip had meticulously crafted, staying aloof so as to not get hurt if things did not go well, collapsed in that moment. He stared into Amanda's eyes. It was as if they had been together all their lives.

"You know, you're much prettier in person than in your pictures..." smiled Philip. Amanda blushed and smiled simultaneously.

"No, I'm not."

"You really are," he insisted.

"Do you want to go to a movie?"

"Sure. What do you want to see?"

"I don't know... you're the guest," said Amanda.

✕

Amanda and Philip entered the movie theater in the middle of the feature, and much to their delight, there were no more than a few people scattered around.

Neither of them paid attention to what movie they chose, but once they got inside the theater, Philip realized it was the same film that he had watched on his failed date with the infamous Marina/Eurydice. But it no longer mattered. With Amanda by his side, nothing that had happened in the past had any more bearing on his life.

"My love," Philip murmured. As they stood in the entryway of the theater, waiting for their eyes to adjust to the darkness, Philip bent and gave Amanda another kiss.

Holding Amanda by the hand, Philip made his way through the crowded theater to a pair of available seats. When they finally sat down, Amanda looked at Philip. She thought of the qualities she saw in him: Tender. Nurturing. Passionate. In the darkness of the theater they both felt excited and embarrassed. Despite already having had intimate conversations by phone and email, trying to find the same level of intimacy in real life was clumsy. In silence, they kept glancing at each other sharing an acute embarrassment.

They had chosen a place in the back row, a location that those who actually want to watch a movie would avoid at all costs. Philip and Amanda would have lots of privacy.

"So…" whispered Philip. "Amanda…" Philip fell silent and began to reach his hand towards Amanda's face, stopping short of touching her, unsure of how she would react. She smiled, took his hand and placed it on her face. She skin was so soft, so warm. It felt like touching heaven itself.

"Can I…?" he asked, unsure if she would know what he was talking about.

"Yes… you can…" she responded.

The next moment, their lips touched. Amanda's kiss was something indescribable. Her mouth was warm, soft, sweet. The way she moved her lips and tongue were so intense.

It was more than mere sexual arousal. It wasn't even something merely physical. There was an intense emotional charge, something that Philip had never before experienced in his life.

Amanda's kiss was wrapped in a cocoon of warmth and purity. Time stood still. The pace of their breathing and heartbeats were now entwined.

*A gateway to heaven...*

Amanda was on fire, kissing Philip's lips and neck. Philip's head fell back limply; his head was spinning. He'd imagined things like this, but never that she would take the initiative.

"I love you, Amanda... I love you so much..."

The fever. The desire. Philip lost all sense of time. It was like a dream. He embraced Amanda, trying to merge her flesh to his, desperately in need of feeling her skin, her body. His hands probed tentatively at her breasts and she shivered and moaned. He realized that it was as much the fear of being caught as it was an actual arousal.

Suddenly, just as he was about to reach the point of no return, the film ended and the lights came up. The few other moviegoers began to walk up the aisle, and Philip panicked a little, while Amanda was still all over him.

"Amanda... please... I can't... I can't..."

She seemed even more aroused by Philip's words. She went on kissing him, deeper and more passionately. "Jesus," muttered

Philip, embarrassed at the seeming exposure. "I'm sorry... I can't..."

Amanda touched his face and kissed him again.

"It's okay."

Though he was a little embarrassed by what had happened, Philip was even more in love with her. He kissed her back, so eagerly that it was even a little painful.

"Ow… Philip, that hurts..."

Philip stopped, feeling even more embarrassed than before. What was happening to him? Since when had the mild-mannered young boy become so wild? His heart was beating fast, but now it was partly from fear. For the first time in his life Philip felt as if he could lose himself.

"Angel..." said Amanda, caressing his face. "It's okay..." Somehow it seemed as if she was able to feel his emotions. A bond had been formed between them. "You don't have to be afraid of touching me... I like your touch." She grasped his wrist gently and guided Philip's hand to her breast. "Here... I... I want you to touch me... here."

He could feel Amanda's heartbeat. Her lips were cold, almost freezing cold. Her hand was shaking as she held his wrist. Philip's other hand touched the soft skin of Amanda's upper arm as gently as possible. He could feel the gooseflesh rising.

"Philip..." Amanda whispered, her eyes closed.

"Yes..?"

"I should tell you that I'm a virgin..."

He hadn't thought otherwise, not even when she was so forward with him. Now Philip's lips were cold as well. She was like a porcelain doll, delicate and fragile. He was so afraid of hurting her. Would he make her bleed if he were to touch her intimately? The expression that was on her face — was it pain instead of pleasure?

After hearing her confession, Philip was unable to go any further. He took his hand off her breast and caressed her face gently. He embraced Amanda, and then they kissed once more, a long, tender kiss.

✕

When they came out of the theater, they already felt and behaved like a couple that had been together a lifetime.

Philip barely recalled later how they found Paul and Suzan again, or going to the car, or the drive to their house. It was as though the entire way, Philip was walking on a pathway made of cloud. Philip finally had reached Pasargada.

✕

Pasagarda.

Manuel Bandeira had written of it half a century ago, in one of Philip's favorite poems. Bandeira was a Portuguese poet and literary critic. He wrote *Paságardae* in 1959, the year Philip's father was born. Despite his credentials as a lawyer, Anthony had never been much of a reader, but Philip loved books from the time he was a small child. By the time he understood the concept of destiny, *Paságardae* was among his very favorites.

Pasagarda was the name of the capitol city built by King Cyrus of Persia in the 6$^{th}$ century BCE. It was also the location of his tomb. When Bandeira wrote, "I'm going to Pasagarda," in a way, he was saying both that he was going to the place he considered his paradise and his ultimate resting place, and that he was going to a place where he would have everything that he had ever wanted.

Philip had found Pasagarda.

✕

Time didn't last long when he was with Amanda. After the movie was over, they went back out into the mall, found her parents, and went back to the car.

✕

Amanda's family lived on a quiet little street, one that almost felt like it was located in a small town. It was the sort of place you would expect to find someone leaving a cherry pie cooling on the windowsill. The air smelled of cinnamon and autumn leaves. Amanda's home was delicate and pretty, just like Amanda herself. Paul pulled the SUV up in the driveway and they all got out.

Philip stood in front of the house, but found himself unable to go any further.

"Philip, what's the matter?" asked Amanda.

"It's nothing… I'm fine."

"Come on in then, Mom and Dad are waiting for you," said Amanda, taking him by the hand. "Come on."

He smiled. "Anything for you…"

They went inside, and there was Suzan, sitting on the couch. The living room was typical modern decor from the furniture to the wallpaper, and yet it felt and looked so special to Philip. It was just as he had dreamed. Even Suzan's piercing eyes couldn't take away Philip's joy. Besides, Paul was there, and in the short time Philip had known him, Amanda's father had proved to be an easygoing person.

"Mom, Dad, would you mind keeping Philip company for a bit? I'm gonna go change," said Amanda.

"No problem, Mandy. It'll be our pleasure," said Paul, inviting Philip to sit on the chair across from him. Paul turned towards him, and despite of the man's calm demeanor, Philip felt like he was about to be interrogated. However, his fears proved to be unfounded, but rather — to Suzan's disappointment — they had a pleasant conversation. Paul asked all Philip all sorts of questions about life in the Big Apple.

✕

"So, Philip, do you live in Manhattan?"

"I wish, but no… I live in Brooklyn at the moment."

Philip caught a sideways glance from Suzan at that.

"Buffalo is an interesting place to live, but it gets too damned cold!" said Paul. "I'd like to pick up and move to Florida, but Suzan's parents and sisters are here. You know how it is."

Philip had always had a habit of arching his back while sitting and then resting his elbows on his knees. It was a way to calm himself while facing tense situations. Then he heard a bell-like voice, and looked over his shoulder to see Amanda returning.

"Daddy, let's take Philip to see more of the city," said Amanda with that graceful smile of hers.

✕

Paul seemed to take pleasure in showing Philip all the sights that Buffalo had to offer, and he spent quite some time doing so. After more than an hour of driving around, Paul decided it was time to take Philip to check in to his hotel.

"Time to hit the Holiday Inn, kid," said Paul while parking the SUV. He laughed and said, "No, actually, you're staying here at the Millennium."

*These guys really want to break me,* thought Philip.

✕

Philip had made his hotel reservation several days in advance. Despite his financial concerns, Philip felt a sense of relief at the idea that he could finally take a shower and get a little bit of rest.

"So we'll head back home for a bit; in the meantime, you can take a shower and change your clothes, but don't get *too* settled in; we'll be back around seven," said Paul with a smile.

Amanda was craving Philip's arms around her. They bid a painful farewell as they knew they would not see each other again for at least a couple of hours.

He entered the hotel lobby, which was well nicely decorated, and walked up to the front desk.

"Good afternoon, sir... would you like to check in now?"

"Yes, please. I have a reservation. McReynolds? Philip McReynolds?"

"Yes, indeed. It's $87.50... Would you like to put that on your Visa or MasterCard?" the smiling young man said.

"Actually, I'm paying cash." He counted out five twenties and the desk clerk gave him back his change.

"Very good, sir." He handed Philip a cardkey. "Room 312, Mr. McReynolds; it's on the third floor."

Entering the elevator, Philip looked up and saw his own reflection in the mirrored interior of the elevator car. He realized that he had a huge smile on his face; it was quite different from the expression he usually wore. It was a sincere smile, and he liked it. The most natural things are so beautiful, he thought to himself.

✕

Philip put his bag on the foot of his bed and got ready for his shower. The shower in the apartment that he and his mother shared was horrible; the water pressure was awful, and the shower head was clogged with whitish calcium deposits. He kept suggesting that they go to a home improvement store to get a new one, but Julia always made the excuse that it was the building owner's responsibility to replace it, which was difficult to argue.

The hotel room's shower, on the other hand, was amazing — an intense blast of steamy water. He stood under it until his fingers were wrinkled, and washed his hair twice with citrus-scented shampoo. He then wrapped himself in a towel and sank down onto the soft mattress of the room's queen-sized bed. If not for the absence of Amanda, it would have been perfect.

Despite all this luxurious comfort, he didn't linger, but got dressed in preparation to be picked up by Amanda and her family.

## 22: THE ASIAN PRINCESS

When they arrived, Philip hurried out to the car; they had brought their other vehicle, a luxuriously appointed Cadillac. As soon as Philip climbed in, he was struck by Amanda's appearance. She resembled an Asian princess. She leaned in to him and hugged him tight, and said to him, "You have such intense eyes!"

Those words left Philip a bit curious: he had always been told that his eyes were more or less expressionless. Since when had they become intense? Perhaps it was at the same time that his smile became sincere.

"It isn't that my eyes are intense," whispered Philip. "Intense is what my feelings are for you."

There, enfolded by the warmth and softness of Amanda, Philip had another flash: Laura, the woman who had delivered the final blow to his parents' already broken marriage, was of Asian descent, and therefore over the last year or so Philip had developed a certain dislike for all things Asian.

Suddenly, none of it mattered any more. Amanda's love was slowly breaking through the darkness of Philip's past. She was like the rain that falls in the desert, nourishing the parched soil, and relieving the thirst of the camels and Bedouins.

All his life, Philip had dreamed of and loved rain. Suddenly he realized that Amanda was this rain.

✕

They stopped at a pizzeria for dinner. As they were getting out of the car, Paul pointed out some of the beautiful buildings and other landmarks in that part of the city. None of it mattered. Philip only had eyes for Amanda.

Soon they were sitting next to each other at the table, their fingers nervously entwined beneath the table, away from the eagle-eyed stare of Suzan. Everything was so perfect, and Amanda so flawless, like a living dream.

After dinner, Paul wanted to show Philip even more of the city. "I'm gonna show you where the hoity-toity rich people of Buffalo live," he said.

I wish I could show you the house I grew up in, thought Philip. It puts some of these to shame.

Paul drove slowly; there was no traffic to speak of, only a very few vehicles on the road. Suzan was soon asleep in the passenger seat, and Paul was also showing signs of fatigue.

The only ones who seemed wide awake were Philip and Amanda. He could see Paul glancing at them now and then in the rearview mirror, making Philip feel a little self-conscious about the situation.

He was so drawn to Amanda, and had a strong desire to kiss her, he knew it wouldn't do for them to make out in the back seat while her father drove.

Philip turned and looked into Amanda's eyes, and saw that her eyes were bleary and misty. He realized that she couldn't see a thing. "Are you okay?" he said quietly. "Are you crying?"

"I'm fine," she said. "I'm just so happy to be with you."

Soon, Philip's eyes were misty too.

✕

It was nearly midnight when they arrived back at the hotel. Suzan was no longer sleeping. The Awakening of the Beast, thought Philip.

"I'll be by to pick you up at about 6:30 in the morning," Paul said.

"That's great," Philip said. "I'll be waiting at the door." His eyes weren't focused on Paul, however, but on Amanda and her beautiful Chinese red dress. They exchanged a look so intense that Suzan could not help but notice it.

"Let's go home, Paul, Brooklyn Boy needs his sleep."

After Amanda's family had left, Philip walked into the hotel lobby. "Can I ask a favor?" he asked the receptionist.

"Yes, of course," the man responded with uncharacteristic sympathy, even for a hotel employee of the hotel.

"Could I get a wake-up call for 5:30 AM?"

"Sure. Oh, and don't forget, we offer a complimentary breakfast starting at six."

"Great. Thank you."

Philip walked toward the elevator, already sleepy. He reached the room just in time to collapse on the bed. Although he hated waking up early, Philip slept with a smile.

✕

Earlier that evening, Anna and Julia had been sitting at an outside table at the Park Slope Starbucks in Brooklyn, talking and watching people walk by. It looked as if it might rain, just the kind of weather that Philip had always thought beautiful. Anna had talked to her friend the lawyer, and had some good news to relay to Julia regarding a scheme to leave Anthony penniless. Now she thought it was the proper time to attempt to solve Philip's problems.

"Wow, it's really cloudy today... you know, it's too bad Philip isn't here. I bet he would like it."

Julia frowned at the mention of Philip's name. "I'm sure he would," she said, "But he's isn't even in Brooklyn. He took off yesterday on a bizarre road trip to meet some random girl he met on the Internet."

"Really?"

"It's true! I'll tell you, the level of ingratitude of that boy is increasing at a rapid pace. I don't know what to do."

Anna regretted even mentioning Philip, and felt her hopes of Julia focusing on the divorce suit fading. She wanted to change the subject, but for Philip's sake, she determined to continue. If she gave up, she knew no one would be able to save Philip from Julia's grasp.

"Where did he go?"

"Oh, my God, you won't believe it. He borrowed your Henry's car and took off to go to Buffalo. Oh, Anna… I tell you ... The boy is crazy ... He even said something about leaving New York."

Anna sat, letting Julia get the entire matter off her chest.

"It's hard, Anna, raising a child, pouring all your love into them, and then having to watch helplessly as he gets himself lost."

Anna saw, at that moment, an opportunity to speak up for Philip. "Julia, you know, if the boy's heart seems to be in Buffalo, wouldn't it be a good idea to let him be there for a while?"

"What do you mean?"

"I mean, let him follow his heart for a while." Despite seeing that she had raised Julia's hackles a bit, Anna went on: "Julia, Philip's been through a lot, what with the divorce, his father not being around much any more… I think he needs some time to forget all that."

"But that's not what I want for him. Pretty soon it'll be time for Philip to start at Brooklyn College… we live so close to it…"

Anna felt a chill run up her spine, and a deep sense of dismay came over her when she heard that. She realized that Julia was hell-bent on keeping Philip under her wing, never allowing him to have his own way. How would the poor kid ever have a life?

"Julia, it shouldn't be about what *you* want. It should be Philip's decision what he does with his life." She paused for a moment, thinking. "If I tell you something, will you promise me not to get offended, and that you'll give it some consideration?"

Julia peered at her best friend silently.

"Look," continued Anna. "I have a cousin in Buffalo. Philip could go to school there, maybe get a scholarship, a part-time job..."

Julia's cheeks were turning pink.

"It'll be good for him to change a little. Go to a new place, meet new people, leave the past behind..."

"Anna, tell me one thing..." Julia's face was crimson now, her eyes wide. "Why would Philip need a change of scenery? And who says he *needs* a change of scenery?"

"Julia, he has a girlfriend in Buffalo. There's nothing for him here..."

"What do you mean? What about me? I'll be alone... abandoned to a dusty corner of the room...?"

"Julia... he's not going overseas, for God's sake, it's a few hours away by car. He needs some time on his own! The way you're acting, you're doing him more harm than good."

Julia was overtaken by a profound indignation. How dare Anna say those things to her? How could she think that Julia was doing anything but good for her son?

Since when would a mother ever harm her child? She'd carried Philip in her womb for nine months... how could Anna think she could ever hurt him? Anna had lost her mind, of that Julia was certain. All a child needed was the presence of his mother. Everything else was expendable.

"Anna, there is *nothing* more beautiful in this world than the love between a son and his mother!"

Anna sighed. She could see there was no reasoning with Julia.

Arriving home, Julia's soul was still consumed by hatred and the feeling of being wronged. "It's all that damned girl's fault," Julia growled while walking in circles.

"He'll see... I'll make Philip remember who is the most important person in his life... he'll remember..."

✕

Finally alone in his room, Philip looked at his cell phone. He had left it charging in his room, partly because the battery had been nearly dead and partly to avoid calls from his mother.

He didn't want to spoil his perfect weekend, but now there was no other way. Suzan would ask him again and again whether he had called his mother, reminding him, "Mothers do care for their children."

As soon as Philip turned his phone on, all hell broke loose. He saw that he had 30 missed calls and nearly 70 text messages.

He checked his voice mail. "Philip, you chose her over me... And I thought I was the most important person in your life... After so much ingratitude, I've decided to find my way out....out of this world... One whore already took my husband, and now another one's trying to take my only son... I can't take it anymore...

"Goodbye, Philip... I hope you can be happy with your new family... Goodbye…"

Philip felt the ground dissolving under his feet, but this time for the wrong reasons. What to do now? Even if he drove back to New York, it would be too late to keep her from doing whatever it was she had planned. He decided to call Aunt Anna.

After ten rings, Anna finally picked up the phone. It was nearly 1:00 AM.

"H… Hello... who is this?" she answered groggily.

"Anna... It's me, Philip…"

"Oh, Philip. Hi. How's Buffalo? Are you enjoying it?"

"It is okay… but… it's Mom... do you know if she's okay?"

"As far as I know… Why?''

"She sent me a lot of texts... I think she… she might have…"

"What?"

"She was talking about killing herself."

"Oh, jeez..."

"Anna, I'm scared..."

"Okay, Philip, don't freak out. I'm gonna call her, and then I'll call you right back."

It only took a few minutes, but it seemed like hours. Finally Philip's phone rang.

"Philip, she's not answering her phone."

"Oh, god..."

✕

Philip drove recklessly towards New York, far exceeding the speed limit, dodging the few vehicles he encountered on his way. He pictured Julia lying dead on her bed. Tears rolled down his face, blurring his vision.

"Get off the road, you son of a bitch!" he cried at the driver of a truck that drifted into his lane. He pulled over onto the roadside, his entire body shaking. He hadn't even had time to say goodbye to Amanda; instead, he had simply left a letter with the receptionist.

*My Princess... I got a disturbing phone call from home and had to hit the road right away in the middle of the night... When I get home, I will tell you more... Sorry, I wish we could have had more time together... We will, very soon.*

*Love,*

*Philip*

# 23: THE HELL WITH JULIA

"What's wrong? Why doesn't he pick up the phone?" Julia kept saying.

"Maybe he's sleeping," said Anna. They were sitting on Julia's sofa, trying to deal with "the Philip crisis," as Julia had dubbed it.

"Who could sleep after getting such disturbing news? He probably hit the road, and it's so late... He has almost zero experience in driving... He didn't think anything of it when he decided to go for a six-hour drive to meet a strange girl... By the way, if he's driving back, that's a good thing. He's coming back where he belongs," said Julia, sipping some hot tea.

"You scared the shit out of me, Julia," Anna said angrily.

Henry sat on the other end of the sofa, even more worried about his best friend than he was astonished by Julia's behavior. *Aunt Julia has always been nuts,* he thought. He was about to call Philip himself, although he knew he was unlikely to answer, when Philip stormed through the front door.

"Mom!"

Philip's eyes scanned the entire room, but saw only Henry and Anna on the sofa and Julia sitting primly in one of the high-backed chairs, sipping her tea. No paramedics were present; Julia wasn't even lying down. And by the look on the faces of those around, there was no doubt that it had been a setup.

"I knew you'd come back, Philip. You came back for your mother…"

Philip didn't say a word. The look on his face said it all.

Henry rose and walked over to meet him. "Phil, bro... take it easy..." he said, touching him on the shoulder. "I know it wasn't right, what she did, but trust me, she's really not in her right mind." He ignored the look that Julia gave him.

Anna was also trying to cool things off, but it wasn't helping.

Philip didn't say a word, but walked slowly towards Julia, in complete silence. She rose, as if expecting a hug.

"I'm getting so tired of this..." Philip said, finally breaking the silence.

"Tired?" Julia felt a flow of indignation running through her veins. "Tired of what? You're always tired, Philip! For your mother you're always tired! But to drive six hours, you're not tired! To leave your mother alone to go visit some strangers, you're not tired!"

"For God's sake, Julia!" said Anna.

"What?! He's my *son,* Anna! My *only* son!"

"More like a pet, I'd say." Henry broke into the conversation.

"Henry..." said Anna.

"Come on... It doesn't take a doctor to see that Aunt Julia is fucking crazy. She made him drive home, late at night, thinking she was dying! That she was gonna kill herself! It was, at the least, completely irresponsible..."

"How *dare* you, you brat!" said Julia in a fit of rage, but Philip interrupted her.

"So, when's the funeral?"

"What?"

"Well, the way you were talking in the messages you left, I was ready to come back in here and find you dead."

Julia stared at him in anger.

"Let's get it over with, and get you buried, once and for all," Philip said.

"Is there someone turning you against your mother? Is it that little bitch? What's *happened* to you? You were always such a good boy, so attached to your mother..."

"Yeah, you're right... maybe I should hang *myself* instead. That's a *much* better idea."

"Oh, god*damn* you! You always were such an ungrateful child! You *never* cared about your mother! Oh, my God, Philip, you're such a disappointment, in *every way!*"

Philip felt his blood boiling. Julia had just forced him to head back home in the middle of the night, and now she dared to lecture him on what a bad son he was? He couldn't take it any longer.

"You implied in those texts that you were going to die..."

Julia stared at him, waiting for what he would say next.

"Actually..." he paused.

"What?" said Julia.

Now Anna and Henry were listening intently as well.

"I wish I'd found you dead when I got back."

"Oh, *Philip...*" Julia groaned like a mortally wounded animal, tears filling her eyes, a vision that angered Philip even more.

"Do me a favor, Mom, and just die! Go ahead and die, so you can quit pissing me off! Do it, for God's sake! Quit threatening to do it and do it. Do the whole fucking world a favor, and *die!*"

✕

Philip left the apartment, slamming the door. It was raining heavily, thunder rumbling in the angry sky. It was the exact sort of weather that Philip loved so much. Despite that, it didn't improve his sour mood. He sought refuge inside Henry's car, and realized as he walked around it that there was a sizable dent in its right front fender. That truck driver had been right to be pissed; another inch and a split second later and Philip might have plowed the little car right into the heavy truck. As it was, he must have sideswiped it and not even realized. He would have to come up with some money to help Henry get his fender fixed.

Philip reached for his cell phone, eager to call Amanda now that morning had broken, but its battery was dead once again.

*"Damn* you, mother...!" cried Philip, collapsing against the steering wheel.

✕

Amanda hadn't been able to sleep that night after they dropped Philip off at the hotel. She kept waking up in the night, thinking about the afternoon and evening that she had shared with Philip; the tenderness, the passion, the desire. She had never experienced anything like it, and it had opened up a whole new world for her. By the time the sun rose, she had already showered and was choosing what to wear that day. She was looking forward to spending another day with the man she loved.

She chose a bra and panties of a deep burgundy lace. She blushed when she realized that she had chosen them because she thought Philip would like them.

Excitement was running wildly through her veins when she and her family arrived back at the hotel.

She went up to the third floor, only to find a maid cleaning the room, and Philip nowhere to be found. "I'm sorry, Miss, but the person in this room left sometime in the middle of the night."

"What? But… that can't be!" She hurried out to the car, in tears.

"What's the matter?" asked Suzan, thinking that Philip had done something terrible to her daughter.

"Philip's gone," said Amanda. "They said he left in the middle of the night."

"I'll find out what's going on," Suzan said. She went inside and inquired at the front desk, only to be told that Philip had left around 2:00 AM.

"I don't understand..."

"Is there a problem?"

"We were supposed to pick him up this morning. I don't know why he would have left in the middle of the night. Did he leave a message or anything?"

"Well, actually, it wasn't my shift. I just came on a few minutes ago. James was the person on duty during the night shift, but I think he may have gone home already. Hold on just a second, ma'am..."

The hotel employee made a couple of phone calls, but his efforts were fruitless.

"I'm sorry, ma'am, I am told he hasn't left yet but I can't find him. Perhaps if you'd like to check back with us in just a little while...?"

Suzan went back to the car, where Amanda was trying to hold back her tears.

"So he's just gone?" asked Paul.

"Yes... it just doesn't make any sense," said Amanda.

"No, it doesn't. Mandy, did you two have a fight or anything?"

"No," said Amanda. "No, everything was perfect." But she was thinking, *Did I scare him off by telling him I'm a virgin?*

"We can wait a little while," said Paul. "The desk clerk who was working last night is around somewhere, but it'll be a bit before they locate him."

"Sure... we can sit here a bit and see if they can find out anything," said Suzan. "Mandy, did Philip call you or text you?"

"No," she whispered, tears welling in her eyes.

"Relax, sweetheart. There has to be a good reason for this."

Amanda was silent.

"Here comes the desk clerk, I bet," said Suzan, indicating a young man in hotel employees' garb who was approaching their car. "The one who checked Philip out. Come on."

The two of them went and asked the hotel employee if he'd been the night clerk. Yes, he had. Yes, in fact, there was a young man who had checked out in the wee hours, and he had, in fact, left a note.

They went into the office and he found it for them. Amanda opened it, afraid of what she would find.

"Oh..."

"What is it?" asked Suzan.

"It wasn't my fault at all," said Amanda.

"Of course it wasn't," said Suzan.

✕

It had been nearly two days since anyone had seen Philip. Julia talked about going to the police, but Anna pointed out that they would likely tell her that there was a 72-hour waiting period before they could take a missing persons report on anyone over the age of 18.

Julia thought about calling Anthony, an idea which upset her greatly — she didn't want to have any contact with him — but, after all, it did make sense. Anthony was his father, and even under the spell of that little Chinese whore, surely he could afford a few moments of lucidity in order to help find Philip.

"Julia..." said Anthony with all the enthusiasm of a bank clerk. "What do you want?"

He was relaxing in a chair, taking in the glorious view from the bedroom window of his house on his newly leased ranch in Montana. The move had nearly broken him, but it was well worth it. *And there were some other perks as well,* he thought, looking at Laura, asleep on his bed.

It was cold in Montana. Nevertheless, Anthony reclined in the chair, clad only in a pair of boxer shorts, sitting in the large leather armchair in front of his king size bed.

Laura lay on her belly, completely naked except for a thin western-print throw. With such a delightful sight available to his gaze, Anthony's humor was much improved. Still, he was unwilling to waste even a single second of his life talking to the woman who had made his life so miserable.

"What happened, Julia?" Anthony asked quietly, almost whispering. He didn't want to wake Laura up, but he could hear the tension in Julia's voice.

"Is Philip there?"

"Philip? Here with me?"

"Yes, that's what just I asked you."

"No, he isn't. Why would he be here? Why would you even ask that?"

"Isn't it obvious? Philip has gone missing."

Upon hearing those words, Anthony felt a shiver run down his spine.

# 24: GIMME SHELTER

In truth, Anna knew exactly where Philip was. She had offered him the sofa in the apartment that she and Henry shared for as long as Philip felt it necessary to avoid his mother.

The big blow-up, as Julia was now referring to it, had occurred on Saturday morning after Philip had driven through the night from Buffalo.

Though Philip had ignored the dozen or more calls he received from Julia on Saturday afternoon, he did answer when Anna called, though grudgingly. He expected her to be sitting on Julia's sofa and that she would tell him how heartbroken his mother was, how sorry, et cetera, et cetera, et cetera.

Instead, when he said hello, what Anna said was, "Hey, kid. Your mom can be a real jackass, can't she?"

"Uh… yeah."

"You need a place to crash for a few nights?"

"Oh, man… that would be great, Anna."

"Come on over. Your mom doesn't ever have to know. You can stay as long as you feel like you can't stand to be in her presence," she said with a laugh.

He stayed with them Saturday night, Sunday night and Monday night. They talked, they ate together, they laughed. He made arrangements to pay Henry for the repairs to his car's fender. They had a good time. And, of course, Philip called Amanda every night.

He called her when he first arrived at Anna's to explain what had happened.

"Oh, Philip!" she said. "What happened? I've been so worried!"

"Amanda, I'm so sorry. It's been insane here…"

"What happened? Why did you leave in the middle of the night like that?"

"When I got back to my room and checked my messages… my mother had been blowing up my phone the whole time we were gone. She was threatening to kill herself."

"Oh, no!"

"Well… I got back home and she was sitting on the sofa talking to her best friend, talking about me. I should have known better. She ruined our time together."

"Are you serious?"

"Completely. I blew up at her and left. Her friend was on my side, though. She's my best friend's mom… she called me a little later and invited me to stay at their place as long as I needed to. That's where I am now."

"That was sweet of her."

"Yeah… sometimes I wish *she* was my mom instead of my real mother. No, I take that back… I *always* wish that she was my mom."

"That's kind of the way I feel about my mother sometimes, too… except I don't have another mom to go to."

"Well, I am gonna stay here a couple days or so… can I come back up and see you this weekend?"

"I'd like that," said Amanda. Philip could hear her smile.

Four times Julia called Anna. She said reassuring things like "I'm sure he's just fine, Julia. He's nineteen years old. He can take care of himself. He'll come back when he's damned good and ready." Then she winked at Philip.

Finally, on Tuesday he decided that it had been long enough, and he went home. He made it very clear to Julia, however, that he was still angry and he still wasn't speaking to her. She begged him to talk to her, but he only glared at her. This lasted through Wednesday night.

Finally, on Thursday morning, he sat her down at the kitchen table and told her how it was going to be.

"I'm nineteen. I'm not a little boy anymore. You have to stop treating me like one."

"I understand, son. I really do. It's just —"

*"No.* It's not 'just' anything. *No more."*

"I understand," she said quietly. It appeared that the brash, domineering Julia might have been broken at last.

"I'm going back to Buffalo. *Don't call me.* If there are any problems, *I'll* call *you.* Otherwise, I'll see you when I'm damn good and ready.Understand?"

"Yes," Julia said.

✕

The rest of the day was spent quietly. Philip and Julia barely spoke fifty words to each other. He contacted his boss and told him he wouldn't be in the next day. He went to the bank and used Julia's ATM card to get money for the trip. He figured it was the least she could do for him.

He went home and he and Julia ate a quiet dinner, then Philip went to his room and called Amanda.

They had a pleasant conversation, then before hanging up, he said, "I'll see you tomorrow."

# 25: SHUFFLE OFF… Again

The drive back up to Buffalo — this time in Anna's Ford Focus — was uneventful. As he made his way down the main highway, a beautiful snow started to fall. By the time he got to Amanda's house, they had received about two inches of the white stuff.

As before, the Robinsons seemed to feel that they should keep Philip entertained, and they spent most of the day exploring the area. In Paul's four-wheel drive, they had no problem dealing with the snow. They even went so far as to drive to Niagara Falls, which Philip and Amanda stood admiring as the snow fell around them.

Surprisingly, after another enjoyable day spent exploring the area, Suzan insisted that Philip would not stay at the hotel where he'd stayed previously, but in their own home.

"After all, you're practically family now," she said.

Philip felt pleased by the fact that Suzan felt comfortable enough to extend the invitation, and also because by not staying at the hotel he would save some cash, which he could then spend on Amanda. Even though, in some ways, Philip still felt some discomfort in her presence, he seized onto the opportunity to get closer to his "mother-in-law," as he already thought of her. He made the mistake of expressing this feeling to her.

"Mother-in-law? Oh, no... let's not make that leap just yet. You're Amanda's *boyfriend,* not her husband," Suzan replied in what Philip suspected was only mock irritation.

"All right — *nearly*-mother-in-law," he said, forcing a smile on his face, which became much more difficult when he learned that Amanda would be sleeping in her parents' room while Philip slept in her bed. *I thought they had a guest room,* he thought.

"Sorry, Philip, but our home is pretty small. You'll be in Amanda's room and she'll stay with us," said Suzan.

*I could sleep on the sofa in the living room, or on the floor...* he thought. However, he didn't reply or try to argue. Once they offered him their hospitality, there was nothing he could do but abide by the decisions made by the lady of the house — especially when Suzan proved to be extremely formidable in the leadership position.

Amanda was wearing a pair of floral print pajamas, which Philip found just as lovely as anything he'd seen her wearing. Her breasts seemed free and unrestrained under the white cotton fabric, and he had to force himself not to stare.

"Come to bed, Amanda," said Suzan in a tone slightly more urgent than normal.

"Oh, mother... I'll be there in a minute," Amanda answered impatiently.

"Don't be long, Mandy... your young man needs his sleep."

Amanda looked at Philip with annoyance on her face, then smiled and whispered to him, "I'd better go with her." She smiled again with a malicious glee in her eyes. "But if you're up to it, I can steal the car keys and we can make a quick getaway later."

"Love to," said Philip with a smile, "But how would I ever face your parents again?"

She stood looking at Philip, smiling slyly. Philip smiled back. It was as if they had found buried treasure. Three times Suzan called out, but the words were unintelligible. Finally, Amanda called to her, "I'll be right there, Mother!" she lowered her voice almost to a whisper. "Oh, that *witch.*" She ran to Philip and kissed him once, twice, three times, and disappeared into the other room.

Philip walked into Amanda's bedroom and closed the door. After turning out the lights, he lay down and buried his face in her pillow, inhaling Amanda's perfume. Her sheets and even her mattress were impregnated with the sweet scent.

Philip's eyes remained closed as he imagined Amanda, rolled in bed surrounded by her sheets, clutching her pillow. He held the pillow to himself as if he was holding Amanda herself.

After some time had passed, when he felt as if he had absorbed the scent of his beloved into himself, Philip lay looking at the ceiling, where there were luminescent star stickers pasted meticulously in the shapes of the Big Dipper, Orion, and other constellations. When the lights went out, it was as if the ceiling was no more and he could see the sky.

Philip felt as if he were in a magical land, surrounded by sheets and pillows that smelled like Amanda, contemplating a starry sky. There was no doubt that he was, indeed, in Pasagarda.

"Am I dreaming? Is all of this really happening?" Philip asked himself quietly as a tear ran down his face, staining Amanda's pillow. It was a tear of joy.

X

Suzan woke up early. Philip, on the other hand, did not wake until he heard sounds coming from the kitchen. He got up, left Amanda's room and walked towards the source of the noise, wrapping his arms around his torso, rubbing them.

"Is it too cold for you, Philip?" asked Suzan with a smile.

No matter what Suzan did, Philip took it as a form of mockery or a sort of aggression. He disliked her more and more as he saw the overwhelming similarities between her and Julia.

Then he remembered the alleged suicide attempt that Julia had pulled during his first trip to Buffalo, when she felt "abandoned." If these women had so much in common, would Suzan threaten to kill herself as well?

"Good morning, Mrs. Robinson," Philip smiled, ignoring the joke about the cold.

"Good morning, Philip. Did you sleep well?"

"Yes, I did, thank you very much."

"Was the bed comfortable enough? Maybe Mandy's bed is too small for a *big man* like you." Suzan smiled but at the same time gave him that 'detective stare,' as if she was trying to size him up.

"I'm not really that big a man," said Philip.

"You're much taller than Paul, so either you're tall or he's very short," she said.

The not-so-friendly greeting was promptly cut short by the sound of the microwave beeping. Noticing Philip's silence, Suzan softened her tone.

"We bought some frozen pizzas yesterday for your visit. We were planning to have them for dinner tonight, but since we'll be eating out, they're available for breakfast or for snacks. I hope you like pizza. We bought a lot of them."

"Actually, I do. I like it a lot," Philip replied.

For a moment, Suzan seemed less diabolical and perhaps even motherly as she piled his plate high with hot, fresh slices of pizza.

"I think that's plenty, Mrs. Robinson," said Philip after several slices.

"Come on, Philip, you're too skinny," said Suzan as she added two more slices to Philip's plate.

When his stomach was about to explode, Amanda entered the kitchen.

"You'll go to church with us on Sunday, won't you? It's all decorated for Christmas, and I'm singing a solo."

"Oh!" said Philip. He hadn't been to church since his grandmother took him when he was small, but he was looking forward to hearing Amanda sing. "Of course I will."

✕

The weekend passed quickly as Philip and Amanda spent time together, and soon it was Saturday night.

Amanda's parents were the religious type; they were very keen churchgoers, although Philip thought that some of Suzan's behavior wasn't what you would expect from a religious person.

Due to her beautiful soprano voice, Amanda had been recruited to be part of the church choir when she was only fourteen. Suzan loved to talk about how beautiful Amanda's voice was with a note of pride in her voice, and if allowed she would go on forever. Tonight, however, she was interrupted by the doorbell.

It was Mrs. Patterson, a longtime friend.

"Hello, Suzan! I just baked a couple of cherry pies, and I know how much Amanda loves them, so I decided to bring one for her. Oh, well, you know, for you and Paul as well."

"Oh, come in," Suzan said. "We have a guest I'd like you to meet."

"Really?"

"Yes, Amanda has a *boyfriend* now," Suzan said, her tone conveying a slight but detectable note of displeasure.

"Well, I think it's about *time* she had one, don't you?"

Philip could hear the two women's voices from the other room and felt a bit uneasy.

*I feel like a circus freak on display.*

The ladies entered the living room where Philip sat. Mrs. Patterson was an older lady with curly silver hair and such heavy glasses that it seemed as though they would slide off the bridge of her nose and go crashing to the floor at any time.

"You must be Amanda's boyfriend," she said with an extremely tender smile.

"Doesn't take too much to notice it, the way he hangs on her," Susan said.

Philip gave her a sideways glance. He turned his focus back to Mrs. Patterson. "Yes, ma'am," he said graciously. "My name is Philip."

"Oh…" Mrs. Patterson laughed. "Suzan, it's natural for them to only have eyes for each other. They're in *love.*"

"I suppose so," said Suzan.

"Oh, now, Suzan, don't be like that. I can still remember when you and Paul were the same way," Mrs. Patterson smiled.

This seemed to disarm Suzan. Her face darkened and Philip saw a look on her face that frightened him a little.

"So Amanda is going to sing in the choir at church tomorrow morning, isn't she?" asked Mrs. Patterson.

"She sure is, and as always, she'll do beautifully," replied Suzan.

"Well, I hear cherry pie is very good for the vocal cords," Mrs. Patterson winked to Amanda. "And you, my dear boy, should have some as well, just because. What did you say your name was again?"

"It's Philip."

"It's very nice to meet you, Philip. You'd best take good care of Mandy. She's a very good girl."

"Oh, I will, Mrs. Patterson, I will."

✕

The church wasn't far, just a quick car ride. In the back seat, as always, Amanda was on Philip's arm like a child seeking care and protection, and Suzan kept an eagle eye on them. Still, she seemed less fierce this time than she had previously.

Philip closed his own eyes for a moment, and suddenly he could see in his mind the last argument he'd had with his mother. He opened them and decided that staring at Suzan was more bearable than that.

✕

"Take good care of my Mandy, Mr. New Yorker."

"Of course I will, Mrs. Robinson."

They went their separate ways, Amanda toward the choir room with Philip following, and Paul and Suzan toward the narthex of the church to mingle with friends and drink coffee before the service began.

Walking down a hallway toward the choir room, it didn't take more than a couple of minutes before they were greeted by an altar boy who seemed to be rather familiar with Amanda.

"Hey, Mandy, it's been a while. Ready to sing today?"

"Hey, Randy. I sure am. I've been doing the vocal exercises that Kevin recommended."

"So your voice must be at its peak!" Randy said.

"We'll see," Amanda laughed.

Philip felt a sense of uneasiness at this. Who was this guy Randy and how dare he talk to his Amanda like that? Where the hell did he come from? How long had they known each other?

"Yeah, her voice is going to be great. She had her secret recipe just last night," said Philip, breaking into the conversation. He and Randy looked at each other for a moment, as if they were each thinking the same thing: *Who the hell are you?*

"Secret recipe? And what's *that,* if I might ask?" Randy said, breaking the moment of tense silence.

"Cherry pie," Philip said knowledgably.

"Never heard of that as a —" Randy started to say.

"That was just a joke that Mrs. Patterson likes to make," Amanda interrupted. "My *real* 'secret' is warm tea with honey and lemon."

"Giving away secrets, now, are we?" Randy smiled. He looked at Philip. "So… you're a friend of Mandy's? I don't recall meeting you before."

"I'm Philip. I'm Amanda's boyfriend," said Philip with just the slightest bit of a glower.

"Oh, hey, congrats, man. I didn't know."

"We just recently started dating," said Amanda with a smile.

"Well, my congratulations once again to the both of you, and it was very nice meeting you, Philip. 'Scuse me, but I've got to get ready for the service to start."

Amanda noticed Philip staring after Randy as he walked away. "Philip," she said. "You seriously don't have to be jealous of him."

Philip looked at her. "I'm not."

"Of course you are, silly. It couldn't be more obvious if you carried a giant poster board that said I'M JEALOUS and painted yourself green. And besides, there's nothing for you to worry about. Randy's one of my best friends…" Philip's brow knotted up at this. "But he's gay. He came out over a year ago, and came to our church after his old one kicked him out."

Philip was silent, not knowing what to say.

Amanda smiled and said, "I love you."

"I love you, too."

"Philip... I want to be with you forever."

"Really?" Philip smiled involuntarily.

"Yes, really. Forever. For all eternity."

"Then here," he said. "Wear my ring." He brought a piece of gold ribbon out of his pocket and tied it around Amanda's left ring finger. "I found this ribbon on that table. Will it serve until I can get you a real one?"

Amanda smiled. "Yes, Philip. It's perfect."

When it was time for the service to begin, Philip found his way to a pew in the sanctuary. He was impressed by the décor. He had expected a traditional cathedral with dark wood and a huge pipe organ. This church was different than any that he had ever seen — not that he'd seen a lot of them. Instead of an organist, there was a small band including a keyboard player, guitarist, bass player and drummer. The walls of the sanctuary were glass and native stone. The pews were made of metal painted a rich burgundy, with cushions of the same color; the pulpit seemed to be made of Plexiglas, and there was a huge piece of fabric art on the wall behind it woven with iridescent rainbow stripes and an enormous dove that seemed to be flying downwards out of an azure sky. It was bordered on the sides and bottom with a golden binding. Philip thought that he might be able to deal with going to church at a place like this.

The pastor stood up to welcome everyone. Philip stole a look at the program that an usher had given him as he entered the sanctuary and saw that it said that this was Holy Light Episcopal Church. The senior pastor's name was Father John Williams.

"Good morning," Father Johnny said, smiling.

"Good morning!" echoed the congregation, catching Philip by surprise.

"I'm Father Johnny, and I'd like to welcome you this morning to Holy Light. Let the light of Christ envelop you this morning, touch you, and heal you. Whatever your need today, we hope you'll find it this morning. Amen?"

"Amen," repeated the congregation.

"This morning our choir and band has a wonderful anthem for us this morning. The soloist will be Miss Amanda Robinson, and, as always, they're being directed by Brother Kevin Lancaster."

A younger man stood and positioned himself in front of the choir. Amanda stood, smiling, and took a microphone off its stand. The leader nodded at the band members, and the drummer softly clicked off an introduction.

The song began with a soft chord progression on the keyboard, which Philip realized was being played by Randy. The bass came in, playing a descending figure; then Amanda opened her mouth. Philip sat there amazed. *She has the voice of an angel.*

*"Bring a torch, Jeanette, Isabella,*
*Bring a torch, come swiftly and run!*
*Christ is born, tell the folk of the village,*
*Jesus is sleeping in His cradle, ah, ah,*
*Beautiful is the mother, ah, ah,*
*Beautiful is her Son."*

The guitarist and drummer joined in, adding a gentle pulse to the music. Now the choir added their voices:

*Hasten now, good folk of the village,*
*Hasten now, the Christ Child to see.*
*You will find Him asleep in a manger,*
*Quietly come and whisper softly,*
*Hush, hush, peacefully now He slumbers,*
*Hush, hush, peacefully now He sleeps.*
*Bring a torch, Jeanette, Isabella,*
*Bring a torch, come swiftly and run!*
*Christ is born, tell the folk of the village,*
*Jesus is sleeping in His cradle, ah, ah,*
*Beautiful is the mother, ah, ah,*
*Beautiful is her Son.*
*Beautiful is the mother, ah, ah,*
*Beautiful is her Son.*

Philip expected a solemn transition to the part of the service where the pastor took over and preached for an extended period of time, but much to his surprise, the congregation began to applaud. Here and there he heard people call out, "Amen!" and "Praise God!" It was unlike any church experience he could remember ever experiencing.

# 26: KASUMI

*1998*

Ito Kasumi (伊藤藤霞) was eighteen years old, a graduate of Sado High School on Sado Island (佐渡島), Japan. She had plans to work for a year and then attend Niigata University, hoping to earn a degree in Psychology.

On this spring day, she had just left the offices of Nagano Broadcasting Systems in the city of Nagano, interviewing for a receptionist's position, and was going to a nearby Freshness Burger restaurant for cake and coffee before taking the train to Niigata, where she would then catch the ferry back to Sado.

She placed her order, paid and took her food to one of the small tables. As she nibbled at the delicious cake, she glanced across the room and saw a broad-shouldered man, a Westerner, sitting at another table, eating a hamburger. She was rather embarrassed to realize that he was looking directly at her.

He was wearing a dress shirt and tie, slacks, and a lightweight jacket. He had dark hair and a thick beard, and eyes so dark he might as well have been Japanese.

He nodded at her, and she felt a warm flush come to her cheeks. She quickly looked down and continued to eat her cake, thinking, "I must hurry and go before someone thinks that we were exchanging glances."

Too late. Suddenly, she looked up to realize that he was standing in front of her. He bowed in the Japanese style.

"Forgive me," he said in impeccably accented Japanese. "I could not resist speaking to you, as I was captured by the trap of your beauty."

Kasumi said nothing, but smiled and looked down.

"I am Alonso Fausto Hidalgo Muñoz, originally of Madrid, Spain, although I am a permanent resident of New York City. I am here in Nagoya for a year, teaching English at Meijo University. I am aware that this is forward, but would you do me the honor of accompanying me to dinner tonight?"

✕

That was how it began. Before the month was out, the two were seeing each other virtually every night. Practically everyone on Sado Island was whispering about the young girl who was being courted by the *gaijin*.

Before long their relationship became more serious. For more than six months this went on, and then, predictably, there came a time when Kasumi began to wonder why her typical, natural monthly cycle that had always been quite regular was late in coming. One day when she was in Nagoya, she obtained a pregnancy test and followed its instructions early the next morning.

When she broke the news to Muñoz that evening, his face was grave. "I must go now, to give this situation some thought and plan for our future." He saw her to the train and sent her on her way home.

✕

The next afternoon, the telephone rang. It was Muñoz.

"My love," he said. "You know that you mean more than the world to me, but… at this point in my life, I am not in a position to make a commitment to any*one* or any*thing*. I must return to New York soon, where I have business waiting. I hope that you can understand."

The line disconnected, and she sat stunned for several minutes, holding the big black telephone receiver that had once been her grandmother's and was now her father's and mother's.

Finally she hung it up, and a sob escaped her throat. Large, wet tears began to roll down her cheeks and soon she was crying and shaking.

Mrs. Ito came in and sat next to her, placing her arm around her and tutting to calm her. She had known all along that the *gaijin* would hurt Kasumi, but the girl refused to listen. The young never think their elders know anything.

"I'm sorry, Mother, I'm so sorry! I should have listened to you…"

"It's all right, my girl. He's gone; that's all that matters."

"No, no…" she sobbed. "You don't understand —"

She looked into her mother's eyes, and Mrs. Ito knew the truth.

"He does not want a child or a wife yet," Kasumi said.

"Of course he doesn't," her mother said coldly. "All he wanted, he got from you already."

Kasumi's face fell.

✕

Over the next six weeks or more, Kasumi's belly began to grow larger. There was no word from Muñoz, and she decided that she was well rid of him. *A lesson learned,* she thought.

Then one day, unbeknownst to Kasumi, a letter arrived for her. Her mother opened it, read it, and promptly burned it.

Six weeks later, another one arrived. The letter was, of course, from Muñoz, just as the first one had been. This one included a cheque for a substantial amount.

"I apologise for having left so abruptly," wrote Muñoz. "I was not thinking clearly. I was shocked, and confused, though I do not know why I was either one.

"I would like to help pay for the medical expenses associated with the child's birth, and for your care; perhaps at some point in the future we can attempt to pick up the pieces and resume where we left off."

Kasumi's mother slipped the cheque into her handbag and, just as the with the first, burned the letter.

Letters continued to arrive every few weeks, and each time, Kasumi's mother kept the cheques and burned the letters. A few months later, the time came; it was February, and the snow was deep on Sado Island. One evening, Kasumi began having contractions — mild ones at first, but they quickly increased in strength. There was no way to travel, so Kasumi's mother and a neighbor woman prepared to deliver the baby while their husbands sat in the living room, smoking cigars, talking and laughing.

A mere three hours later, a baby girl had come into the world. Kasumi was sleeping, exhausted, when her mother went to the telephone and dialed the international operator. She asked to be connected to the New York number that she had written down from the last letter that she had received from Muñoz.

"Hello?"

*"Konichiwa,"* Kasumi's mother said.

*"Konichiwa,"* Muñoz responded. "How is she?"

"She is sleeping. The labor was not long but she is exhausted."

"And the child?"

"A girl."

✕

They made arrangements for Muñoz to travel to Niigata and pick up the baby. They would do it while Kasumi was sleeping. She would never know until it was too late.

The baby, still nameless, was just two days old when Muñoz flew in from New York to spirit her away to her new home in America. At approximately the same time that his plane was lifting off from LaGuardia, on the other side of the world, Kasumi — ashamed, estranged from her parents and neighbors, and at a loss as to what action she should take — slipped silently out of the back door of her family's home and carefully made her way to the hill that formed the scenic vista behind the house, quickly losing her slippers and leaving bare footprints up the mountain in the heavy snow.

✕

More than nineteen hours later, after a layover of more than two hours in Seoul, Muñoz made his way out of Niigata Airport and hailed a cab to the terminal where he caught a ferry to Sado.

Through a sequence of miscommunications, Muñoz had neglected to make note of the Itos' telephone number, and all that Mrs. Ito had was the number at Muñoz's apartment. When the Itos realized the necessity of contacting the Spaniard, the only number they had would have rung a landline in an empty apartment in Brooklyn, many thousands of miles from Japan.

After crossing the strait between the main island and Sado, the ferry docked at Ryotsu; he hired a car to take him to Juodo, where he arrived at the Itos' home to find, in front of the Ito residence, the typical Buddhist altar, or *butsudan,* as well as a Shinto shrine, or *kamidana.* He saw that the shrine was covered with white paper, a practice he had heard of before; it was intended to keep out the spirits of the dead who might otherwise sully the shrine. This custom was called *kamidana-fūji*. He knew, simply from what little he had learned over the year he had spent in Japan, that something terrible must have happened.

When Muñoz knocked at the door, the Itos politely answered the door and silently escorted Muñoz inside. He sat solemnly with the Itos as they explained to him just what had happened.

Kasumi had wandered into the cold night, wearing only a kimono and slippers. She had walked out into the field in the back of the house, ascending as she went. It appeared that she had lost first one and then the other of her slippers, and, although no one in the family saw, disappeared into the darkness.

She had never been found, and was presumed dead.

"We will continue to search, day by day, but I know in my heart…" Mrs. Ito paused. Her eyes brimmed with tears.

The two parents looked at each other. Mr. Ito looked out of the front windows of the small house. He had never spoken a word; he intended to remain silent as long as Muñoz was present.

Muñoz dropped his eyes and said, "I hope you both know that I did not intend for this to happen."

"We know you did not. There is pride involved here, but we know it was not malicious on your part. We do not blame you for what she did."

"I owe you both a *gimu* debt, and one that I can never fully repay," said Muñoz.

At this Mr. Ito broke his silence.

"You owe us nothing," he said quietly. "Simply take the child and go, and we are never to hear of you or her again."

There was a short period of silence, and then Mrs. Ito rose, went into the back room and began packing the baby's things. Mr. Ito handed him the paperwork identifying her as Munoz's daughter.

Fifteen minutes later Muñoz carried the child's meager belongings — all of which fit into one small suitcase — and placed them into the trunk of the rental car, returned for the child, and her carseat, strapped her into the car, and left the house.

He got a hotel room in Ryotsu. They spent the night there, where he fed the baby and watched over the tiny child until she fell asleep.

She had been utterly rejected by her grandparents, simply because her father was a *gaijin* and she was a *haafu,* or half-blood.

The next day Muñoz and his daughter took the fourteen-hour flight back to New York City. She slept most of the way; Muñoz fed her with a bottle, holding her clumsily but lovingly. An older woman in the next row smiled and said the baby reminded her of her own daughter, many years ago. She helped to bottle-feed her. When asked what the baby's name was, Muñoz smiled and said, "We actually haven't decided yet," which was, in fact, the truth.

# 27: AMERICA

*1998*

"What was I thinking?" Muñoz said. He was sitting across the room from his friend Anthony McReynolds and his wife, Julia, who was holding the baby in her arms. "She is my responsibility, but how can I raise a tiny child alone?"

"You could always get married," Anthony said with a sly smile. He had known the Spaniard for several years; Anthony had wandered into the older man's used book store out of curiosity, looking for interesting books of significance, and left having made a new friend.

Muñoz gave a grimace. "You say that with the casual abandon of a typical American," he said. Look what just happened. I allowed myself to carelessly fall in love with a woman —"

"A *girl,* from what you described," interjected Julia with a slight look of disapproval. She wasn't sure of the antiquarian's exact age, but she knew he was at least a few years older than Anthony, and her husband was now 39 to her 37. From what Muñoz had described, the girl he had become involved with had been just eighteen years old. She shook her head slightly.

Anthony glanced at his wife. She was statuesque, blonde, blue-eyed; intelligent, but right now he wished she would simply keep her mouth shut. It might have been a mistake to bring her with him today. He probably should have come alone.

"So," said Anthony. "This is a bit of a tender subject, I realize, but… have you considered putting her up for adoption?"

The two men exchanged looks. It was the truth; Muñoz wasn't cut out to be a father, at least not at this point in his life. His work took up all his time. The year he'd spent teaching in Japan had been a bit of an adventure, but now he was ready to get back to the 20,000 or so volumes of literature, history and other objects of fascination that made up Muñoz Antiquities.

"You could arrange this for me?"

"Yeah," said Anthony. "It's not my usual thing, but it's just like any other sort of legal paperwork. There are agencies where I can find out about couples who are seeking to adopt a baby, and all I would need to do is arrange for you to meet and write up the documents."

There was a long pause. Muñoz stood and walked over to Julia, now rocking the infant gently in her arms. She and Anthony had a son, just a year or two older. Now, he was too big to be cradled in her arms like this. She missed the feeling, and for just a moment she had the impulse to say that she and Anthony would take the tiny little girl as their own. But no, that would pose all sorts of issues with emotional ties. Best that she should go to a couple who could devote their full measure of love and attention to her, and where Muñoz would not be tempted to continually watch her as she grew.

Muñoz nodded slightly to Anthony.

"All right, then," said the lawyer. "I'll make some calls."

A bit less than two weeks later, the little girl was placed in the arms of Suzan Robinson. She and her husband Peter had been married for five years and had been unable to conceive. Tests had shown that Peter's sperm cells were not properly motile. The doctors had told them that while it was possible they'd be surprised with a child of their own one day, it was unlikely, and that they might consider adoption, which is what they had done. Now they sat in the modest offices of Anthony McReynolds, Attorney at Law, in Brooklyn, preparing to sign the paperwork that would allow them to take their new daughter home to Buffalo. When asked, they said yes, they would welcome Fausto Muñoz to be present as the final paperwork was signed.

"Have you decided on a name?" Muñoz asked.

They glanced at each other, then looked at Anthony and at Muñoz.

"We're going to call her Amanda," said Peter.

# 28: JIGSAW

Julia sat on her bed, staring at nothing. Her ungrateful son had gone to see his little whore of a girlfriend again, in…

Suddenly a puzzle piece fell into place. *Amanda. Buffalo.*

She shook her head. *No, no possible way. It can't be.*

She laughed to herself, for the first time in a long time.

*I knew we should have adopted her ourselves.*

# 29: HOME AGAIN, HOME AGAIN

Philip had returned home after spending three days in Buffalo with Amanda. They still had not had the privacy that they needed to become truly intimate; both of them were still virgins, but that didn't bother Philip. He knew the time was coming.

He parked in front of Anna and Henry's place to drop off Anna's car keys as well as to thank her for her assistance the week before. Neither Anna nor Henry were home, so he called Anna's work number.

"Hello?"

"Hi, Anna."

"Philip! How are things?"

"I'm good. I just wanted to let you know that I'm back from Buffalo. I stopped by your place, and I'm leaving your keys on your kitchen table. I want to thank you for everything."

"Oh, that's no problem. I'm glad I was able to help. Did you have a good time?"

"I really did."

There was a slightly uncomfortable pause.

"Philip… have you called your mother?"

"No… not since I saw her Thursday night."

"You really should give her a buzz. She's been so worried. She was threatening to call the state police, but I talked her out of it. I finally had to tell her that I'd given you a place to stay for a few days until you both cooled down. I know she was being ridiculous, but you blowing up at her and saying you wished she would die… well, that wasn't the right way to handle things."

"I know. I'm sorry," said Philip.

"Philip, I've known your mother since high school…"

"Yeah, I know."

"She goes off the deep end sometimes, but she always means it for the best."

"I know that too."

"And she really does love you. She's going through a hard time right now, what with the situation with your dad…"

"Yeah. I wish she understood that I need for her to turn loose of me. I'm grown now. I need to have a life."

"I understand that."

"I'll head home now, and she and I will talk. Can I call you if I have trouble with her?"

"You know you can."

Philip smiled and thought, not for the first time, that he desperately wished Anna was his mother. *That would make me and Henry actual brothers,* he thought as he walked out to the bus stop.

The bus ride was not far, but he almost fell asleep and very nearly missed his stop. He woke just in time, pulled the stop cord, and hopped off a couple of blocks from the apartment.

He went up the steps outside and into the building, stopping to get the mail, and sorted through it as he went up the stairs. Bills, bills, advertising circulars, and more bills, most of which were addressed to his father. It caused a twinge of pain in his chest to still see ANTHONY R MCREYNOLDS on the billing. He got his keys out and unlocked the door.

Inside, it was very quiet.

"Mom?" he called out. There was no response.

He tossed the mail on the kitchen table and dropped his knapsack on the floor.

"Mom, it's me. What are you doing?"

The apartment was completely silent. He decided she had probably gone shopping, but he wondered at the fact that Anna had been at work. Normally if his Mom went shopping, she went with Anna.

He found himself yawning. The drive back from Buffalo had been long. All he wanted to do at this point was to lie down and take a...

No. He needed to check on his mother, the crazy old bat. As much of a pain in the ass as she was, he loved her and he had to make sure that she was all right.

He knocked lightly on her door. "Mom? It's Philip."

The door swung open slightly. He stuck his head inside. Then he froze.

There, lying on the floor, was his mother. She was as pale as the chiffon curtain that was drifting in front of the open window.

*"Mom!"* Philip cried out. He rushed inside and grabbed her wrist, his ear to her lips. He could hear faint breath sounds, and felt a fluttery pulse. *Goddamn you, you stupid woman. Goddamn you.* He grabbed the telephone from her bedside table, and when he did, he noticed the open bottle of diazepam as well as the bottle of Vodka there. Philip was pretty sure that was not a good combination and dialed 911.

911: "Nine one one, what is the nature of your emergency?"

PHILIP: "I just came home and found my mother unconscious. I'm pretty sure she's OD'd on Valium, and may have had some vodka as well."

911: "We'll dispatch an ambulance right away…"

It was only a few minutes before they arrived and Julia was carted away to the hospital. A panicked Anna arrived shortly thereafter. She and Philip headed to Woodhull Medical Center, where Julia had been taken. A nurse ushered them to the Emergency Room waiting area, and it wasn't long before a tall female doctor with a Nigerian accent met them.

"You are relatives?" she said.

"I'm her son," said Philip.

"Very good. Your mother is going to be just fine. We pumped her stomach to remove whatever was still there, and administered activated charcoal to try to prevent as much of the drug as possible from being absorbed into her body. It was a near thing, but we believe she is going to be all right."

Philip heaved a sigh of relief. Despite the anger he had felt at his mother, he felt relieved that she was going to be all right and guilty that she had been driven to this act in the first place.

"You're exhausted, Philip," said Anna. "I'll stay here and wait for any news. You go home and get some sleep."

"I can't do that," said Philip. "This is all my fault."

"No," Anna replied. "This isn't your fault. It's her own fault for overreacting. Go home, or I'll spank you like I did when you were seven. Do you remember that?"

Philip did remember. Anna had caught him and Philip stealing money from her purse and spanked the both of them. She'd spanked him like neither of his parents had ever done. He knew she was teasing — she wouldn't spank him now; he was nineteen years old, for pete's sake — but still, the memory of it was enough to put him off.

"Okay, Aunt Anna," he said. "I promise, I'll go home and rest."

But he didn't. He went to Badi's.

# 30: TROUBLE IN PARADISE

Badi smiled at Philip as he always did, the broad, genuine smile that Philip loved to see, but the look on Philip's face turned that smile into a look of concern.

"What is the matter, young Philip? Your face has a look of worry."

"It's my mother," said Philip. "She tried to kill herself while I was gone." He slid into one of the chairs. "You still have my information, right?"

"Yes, of course," said Badi. Philip had become such a regular customer that Badi had assigned him a permanent ID and password.

In mere moments, Philip was online and typing a message to Amanda. They had generally stopped using e-mail except as a backup method of communication, having discovered that instant messaging services were much more immediate and gratifying.

- ***Are you there?***

There was a brief pause, then:

- **Yes. Hi.**

- ***I have some bad news.***

- **What? What's wrong?**

- ***It's about my mom.***

- **What? What's wrong?**

- ***She tried to kill herself while I was gone.***

- **OMG! Is she OK?**
  - *She's in the hospital. They say she's gonna be OK but it was scary.*
- **Why did she do it? Is it because of ur dad?**
  - *I don't think so. She has a lawyer and stuff. I think it's more because of you and me.*
- **Oh, no.**
  - *Yeah. I may not be able to see you for a while.*
- **What? But why?**
  - *Well, you see what happened. I almost lost my mom. That's something I am having to deal with.*
- **I understand. But why would that make you say that we shouldn't see each other?**

There was a long pause.

  - *You wouldn't understand this. You still have both of your parents.*

There was another pause, this time on Amanda's end.

- **Philip... you've seen what I look like. How could you even say that?**
  - *What are you talking about?*
- **Do I look like my parents?**
  - *I don't...*
- **I know you aren't as dumb as you're acting.**

Philip paused, offended for a moment.

  - *What do you mean by that?*
- **Philip... I'm half Japanese. I'm adopted.**
  - *I guess I just never thought about it before.*

- I was adopted by my parents when I was just a few days old.

    - *Where did you come from?*

- I don't know exactly. All I know is they adopted me through an agency of some kind.

    - *It doesn't matter to me.*

- I didn't think it would. What I am saying is you are not the only one with parental issues.

    - *All right.*

- So where does that leave us?

    - *I still need to take care of my mother for a while.*

Another pause.

- So if you think that your mother needs you more than I need you, maybe it's a good thing that we not see each other any more.

Philip's stomach clenched. He hadn't meant to anger her.

    - *Amanda?*
    - *AMANDA?*

There was no response. He took out his cell phone and dialed her number. It rang and rang, and then went to voice mail.

*"This is Amanda. I can't answer your call right now. Please leave me a message."*

He pressed the disconnect button and put the phone back in his pocket with a look of anguish on his face.

# 31: H&P INCORPORATED, PART IV

"I don't know what I'm going to do, Henry. I call, I text, I e-mail, but she won't respond…"

"Have you tried Western Union?" laughed Henry. He saw the look on Philip's face and reconsidered. He knew his best friend was truly heartbroken. "You're really serious about this girl, eh?"

Philip nodded.

"Okay, then. I'll tell you what we're gonna do…"

Henry detailed the finer points of his plan.

Gradually, Philip's eyes lit up and the corners of his mouth turned up, a little at first and then more and more.

# 32: A FAREWELL TO MOM

Philip went home and gathered everything he would need for an extended stay in Buffalo.

Out front, Henry was waiting in the Citroën, keeping it warm. Just as Philip decided he was ready to head out, the thing that he had been most concerned about happened. Julia, apparently unmedicated for once, came padding out of her bedroom.

"Philip?"

"Yes, Mother?"

"Where are you going?"

"You know where I'm going, Mother," Philip answered her crisply.

"When are you coming back?" she asked

"I don't know," He said. "I'm strongly considering the possibility of staying in Buffalo."

"What?"

"I think I'm going to enroll at State University in Buffalo."

There was a dead silence for a moment or two, then Julia looked at Philip and said, "Just like your father, you always get your way."

She turned and went back to her room.

# 33: SCHOOL'S OUT FOR WINTER

It was the last day of school before Christmas break in Amanda's senior year, and in three days she would turn eighteen.

She was sitting in a classroom next to her best friend Tori, pouring out her troubles. "…and I just don't know what I should do," she said. "I love him so much, but he seems like he is *so* attached to his mother… and she sounds so much like *mine*. I'm just not sure it could ever work."

"Lighten up, Amanda," Tori said. "First of all, you're only just about to turn eighteen. You need to spend a few years partying, hook up with a few guys, figure out what you really want in a man. A *man,* not a boy, which is what it sounds like you've got right now. Seriously, I swear, this boy is some kind of freak."

Amanda didn't say a word, but simply smiled her sad smile and shrugged. Class was almost over, and Amanda began to pack her things, carefully putting everything inside her bag.

"When are you going to take it off?" asked Tori, noticing Amanda still wore the "ring" Philip had given her, made of golden ribbon.

"I will… soon," replied Amanda, caressing the band of ribbon.

"You should have done it a long time ago."

Amanda was silent. Then the bell rang, dismissing the class.

The two girls joined the crowd of countless students leaving their classrooms, eager for Christmas break to begin.

"You should check out the hot guys around here. See that one?" said Tori, indicating a tall blond guy. "I used to date him... what a six-pack! Not to mention..." She raised her eyebrows.

"Oh..." came Amanda's unenthusiastic reply.

"You're hopeless," said Tori, already distracted by another guy who was looking at her.

As they left the building, a light rain began to fall, and soon began to get heavier. Amanda thought of Philip, but said nothing, sure she would find herself being criticized by Tori. Besides, she was still mad at him for having the nerve to break up with her via instant messenger. *Who does that?* she thought.

"What the hell is that moron doing, standing out in the street in this rain without an umbrella?" said a male voice in the crowd around them.

"Where?" said Tori, seizing an opportunity to find a new companion for the weekend.

"You see that?" said a nerdy-looking guy with thick glasses. "There's a guy in a blazer out by the sidewalk... he's holding a bouquet of flowers."

"Is he coming from a funeral?" laughed Tori.

"You know, flowers aren't always for funerals…" replied the nerd, whose name was Ray.

"So what, then?"

"I'd love for a guy to bring *me* flowers," said a smiling red-haired girl.

"What for?" said Tori with even greater dismay.

"You know…" said Ray, "Did you ever think that girls like you might be the reason why so many guys never show their romantic side?"

"Not interested, thanks."

"You're kind of an annoying person," Ray told her. "Did anyone ever tell you that?"

"What makes you think I give a rat's ass about what you think?"

"Hey, no need to start a fight," said the redhead. "Besides, I agree with him. Some girls love romance. Why don't you ask your friend," she pointed to Amanda.

"So, what do you think, Amanda?"

There was no reply. Amanda simply stood speechless.

"Does anyone have an extra umbrella? I think the guy with the flowers might be drowning," said Ray.

"Philip…?" whispered Amanda.

"Oh, God, no… for fuck's sake! It's the *freak,*" laughed Tori.

At that moment, Philip began to walk slowly towards the crowd, a huge bouquet of deep red roses in his hands. Amanda felt her heart pounding.

"And here we go again," said Tori. "Let's call the cops."

"Oh, sure. I mean, that guy carrying the bouquet of roses is a lethal threat for sure!" laughed Ray.

Tori was about to say something cruel to him, but froze when Amanda began to walk Philip's direction.

"Where the hell are you going, Amanda?"

No reply came. She simply kept walking towards Philip. Suddenly the whole crowd seemed to stand still, although most of them had no idea what was going on. Now soaked to the skin, Amanda and Philip were close enough to embrace. She took the bouquet when he offered it to her.

"The florist said that red roses mean love, and I want you to know how much I love you, Amanda."

Amanda was silent a moment. Then she said, "Philip, do you have any idea how much you hurt me?"

Philip was silent, staring at the sidewalk.

"Why did you *do* that to me?" She was shouting now, and everyone around had turned to watch her.

"I'm sorry, Amanda… I didn't mean to…"

"To do *what?* To *hurt* me? But you did, Philip. You hurt me very badly!"

Again the silence.

"You broke my heart... do you have *any* idea how much it hurts, what you've done to me?"

Philip looked up at her, his lips moving, but nothing came out.

"I tried, again and again, to find the courage to call you..."

"Amanda —"

"Do you have *any idea* how much it *hurts?*"

Philip took a deep breath, looked straight into her eyes, and said, "Do you have any idea how much pain it causes me to be *apart* from you?"

"Philip..."

"I didn't know what to say." He reached out and touched her face, and began to caress it. She started to pull away, but he ran his fingers through her hair. Amanda closed her eyes. "Your hair is a little longer..." With the other hand, he gently grasped her delicate wrist and led her hand toward his chest. When Amanda touched it, she felt his heart beating fast. "That's because of you..." He brought his face toward hers. "It's *all* because of you."

"What are you doing here, anyway? Did you just come up today?" asked Amanda, barely keeping her eyes open.

"No," he said. "I moved here this weekend. I'll be here forever... just because of you."

She stared into his eyes.

"I love you so much, Amanda…" Their lips brushed together.

"Well, well… it's time for you to back off, you fucking freak," said Tori, grabbing Philip by the arm.

Amanda suddenly opened her eyes, and saw the red-haired girl and Ray standing behind Philip. They had come to support Philip as soon as they figured out what Tori was about to do.

"I think you're the one who should back off," said Ray.

"And who the hell are you to say so, Four-eyes?"

"My name is Ray… *bitch.*"

Suddenly the redhead burst out in laughter. Even Philip, despite the tension, smiled slightly.

"How dare you call me a bitch, you *loser!*" Tori took Amanda by the hand. "C'mon, let's get as far away from this pack of freaks as we can."

"I think that's up to Amanda," said Philip.

By that time, the blond guy, who went by Nick, had been watching the whole scene with amusement. Now he stepped forward in a self-proclaimed act of chivalry. "How 'bout you lettin' *both* these girls alone, asshole?"

Philip ignored him. "Amanda, I…"

Nick continued: "Didn't you hear me? I said *back off!*"

"What you got to do with it, bro?" said Ray, now fully on Philip's side.

"Mind your own business, Specs."

"Take some of your own advice," Philip told him.

"Don't make things no worse for yourself, buddy," Nick said with a sneer.

"Come on, let's at least get out of the rain. We'll both wind up with pneumonia," said Tori. She took Amanda under her wing and hurried her away. In her state of mind, Amanda offered no resistance. As they passed a trash barrel, Tori reached over and grabbed the roses from Amanda's hand and deposited them in the trash.

"I wouldn't get no closer to that girl if I was you, dude," said Nick with a note of defiance in his voice, looking Philip in the eye.

"Oh? And why is that?" said a new voice in the conversation. Nick turned to look and was met by a withering stare from Henry, who had been watching from the car.

"Who are you, his boyfriend?" Nick said with an uncertain snicker.

"More like Amanda's avenging angel," Henry growled. "Now don't fuck with Philip any more if you know what's good for you."

Nick backed away slowly and left the area.

"I'll keep an eye out for that asshole in case he decides to chance coming back."

"Don't worry about him," said the redhead, whose name was Tessa. She smiled at Philip. "Let's go get some coffee to warm us up."

"I know a place not far from here," said Ray. "Meanwhile, you can tell us what the hell that was all about."

"It's kind of a long story…" smiled Philip.

"We're not in a hurry," said Tessa. "By the way, I loved the flowers. It was so nice of you to bring them. I can't believe Tori didn't appreciate them, let alone Amanda!"

They headed off toward the coffee shop: Philip, Henry, Tessa and Ray.

# 34. COFFEE

The four of them sat in a booth, sipping lattes and mochas. Henry had a plain, black Café Americano.

"...and so that's how it happened. I came up here —" Philip began.

"I *brought* him up here..." said Henry.

"Okay, yes. Henry packed up all my meager belongings and moved me here; I enrolled at SUNY-Buffalo and moved into a dorm room, and then I came to see if I could catch Amanda as she left school today."

"And we all saw how well *that* worked out," said Henry.

"Yeah..."

"That Tori is really a piece of work," said Ray.

"She just likes to make other people miserable," said Tessa.

They finished their coffees, and Philip and Henry thanked Tessa and Ray for the invitation.

"If you feel like going out tonight, some friends and I are going to the Tumbling Dice Club," said Tessa. "Come on down. It'll be fun."

# 35. THE TUMBLING DICE CLUB

*Later*

"Come on, man. We need to get you out of here."

Philip and Henry were making their way across the crowded dance floor of a dance club called the Tumbling Dice in Buffalo. Philip had tossed back a couple of Long Island Iced Teas, and — unaccustomed as he was to heavy drinking — was in a state of heavy inebriation that would have caused most nineteen-year-olds to pass out. He hadn't been carded, and neither had Henry, although Henry had volunteered not only to drive Philip to Buffalo but to serve as his designated driver for the weekend and, if necessary, his second in any disagreements that might arise.

Philip had followed Tessa to the club, determined to get Amanda out of his head. He had soon discovered that few of the patrons of this particular club were of age, and what was more, for the most part, the management didn't care.

Philip and Henry had waded into the mass of partiers and soon were dancing with every pretty girl they encountered. Then Philip saw a familiar face.

Tessa, the red-haired girl that Philip had seen outside Amanda's school during his abortive attempt to win Amanda back, with whom he and Henry had gone for coffee, was on the dance floor, shaking her ass and looking hot. He made his way over to her as Henry went to the bar.

"Hi there," he said. "I lost sight of you after we got here."

"Oh, yeah. I'm sorry, Philip. My boyfriend was here."

"Yeah?" he said, his face falling a bit.

"Yeah," she said, "But he went to the bathroom, like, half an hour ago, and I don't know if he's even coming back… d'you wanna dance?"

Philip quickly agreed, and soon they were moving to the rhythm of the music, smiling and having a good time.

After several songs, the tempo slowed to a love ballad, and Philip and Tessa glanced at each other and stepped closer to begin a slow dance.

Tessa smelled like spring flowers. Philip smiled and held her close as the music played, singing about love and togetherness, and how it would last forever.

For a moment Philip thought about Amanda and felt a twinge of conscience, but then he remembered that she was the one who had walked away when he had come to find her, to try to make things right between them.

*"WHAT THE FUCK ARE YOU DOING?"* roared a malevolent male voice, seemingly right in Philip's ear. He felt a strong hand grasp him by the upper arm, and for a moment he didn't know what was going on. He had a flashback for a

moment to Alexander, but no, that was impossible; Alexander was dead.

Then he realized three truths: Tessa's boyfriend had returned from the restroom, he was big — bigger than Alexander had ever been — and he was angry.

Philip felt himself yanked out the slow dance embrace and spun around to face what seemed at first to be a ravening beast. A full head taller than Philip, with shoulders seemingly twice as wide. Philip got the initial impression that he was face to face with a mountain gorilla or a Yeti. Then he realized that his opponent was simply a very large, very athletic young man who was very, very pissed off.

*"YOU DANCING WITH MY GIRL?"* shouted Philip's musclebound assailant.

"Yes… but I'm sorry, man. We were just dancing. No harm, no foul."

Tessa approached Philip, looking nervous and talking to him loudly, trying to be heard over the strident beat of the dance music. She'd been the cause of the earlier disagreement; her boyfriend hadn't liked the way Philip had looked at her, nor she at him.

However, when he saw the size of Tessa's boyfriend — a 6'4", 235-pound offensive lineman for the Lafayette High School Patriots — Henry, who had been watching from the sidelines, decided that wisdom was the better part of valor and urged the drunken Philip toward the nearest exit sign, telling him, "Hey, man — I think we'd better get going."

Meanwhile, the rest of the club was full of people who were still partying and dancing, unaware of the brawl that had nearly erupted only a few moments earlier.

Tessa was trying to say something to Philip, leaning in to be heard, but it was too loud, the alcohol in his blood too much, the angry boyfriend too much of a distraction. She reached out and touched a place on Philip's face, and despite his being so drunk, it hurt. "A bruise," she said. "You didn't have to…"

Henry had seen the tall fellow Tessa had been dancing with earlier approaching from across the room. He didn't look happy. "Philip," he called, trying to sound a warning.

Philip didn't answer. Henry knew he needed air. Fresh air. He steered Philip toward the nearest door, seeking the dull reddish glow of the emergency exit sign. Pushing through the crowd of partiers, they finally made it outside. Henry made sure Philip was stable and went back inside to try to calm the big bruiser.

Soaked in sweat, Philip felt a shiver run across his skin and shrugged. The magical effect of the booze was fading faster than he'd expected.

Still, his head felt too heavy. It seemed as if it were ready to fall off his shoulders and go rolling down the street. Philip thought of hailing a cab, but there were none in sight. He walked to the nearest corner, searching for a taxi, but ended up walking in circles, staggering and talking to himself. His words meant nothing; they were a bundle of random curses, pleas for forgiveness and vows of everlasting love. His eyes were covered by a fog of drunkenness and tears. Suddenly the bruise on his face began to ache, and along with that, his ribs as well.

In the seedy neighborhood where Philip found himself, he was surrounded by bars and clubs, all filled with other young drunks drowning themselves, as well as their sorrows, in mugs, glasses and bottles of beer, wine, or scotch. At one joint that advertised itself as a Tiki bar, a few opted for hollowed out pineapples, available for a few extra bucks, from which they sipped fruit flavored rum concoctions through long, thin straws. None of them looked outside; none of them were able to see Philip in his pursuit for a cab, getting dangerously close to the street — not until it was too late. A small group, ready to take the party homeward, came spilling out of the Tiki bar just in time to see Philip stumble into the narrow street. One of them cried out, "Watch out!" as loudly as someone who is fairly inebriated could be expected to call, but not as loud as the screech of tires squealing on asphalt as the cab driver tried to stop his vehicle. The sound shocked the rest of the drunken partiers sober. Immediately afterward there was a dull thump, like a trash bag being tossed into a dumpster.

Philip felt as if his body was being swept up by a whirlwind. One moment he saw the heavily clouded sky, darkened by the mantle of the night. Rain was falling like a deluge now. In the next moment all he saw was blackness. A sense of peace came over him, though his body was broken and a trickle of blood dripped from his mouth and grew thicker with every breath he took. Philip lay on the asphalt, gazing towards the sky. In his haze of confusion, he saw a light-haired girl running towards him, crying. It was Amanda.

She knelt by his side and frantically began to touch his face and torso as if she was trying to heal him by her very touch. She spoke to him tearfully, whispering low, so low that one of the others gathering around could make out what was said. But Philip, for whom the words were intended, didn't understand much of what she said either; the darkness was now encompassing him eternally. He felt the soft touch of Amanda's hand, and the tears dripping from her eyes onto his wretched face.

"I love you, Amanda... so much..." he murmured.

Then he blinked, and realized it was Emma Bovary hovering over him, her eyes brimming with tears just as on the day of her father's funeral.

He blinked again. No, he had been mistaken; it was Amanda after all.

"Philip... I love you, too... I love you!" Amanda's voice dissolved into sobbing. All she could do now was utter a single cry as a peaceful smile came to Philip's lips.

"What did he say?" muttered one of the people in the gathering crowd to the young woman who was kneeling over him. She was a registered nurse who happened to be at one of the clubs with a group of friends, and she was checking him for injuries.

"I'm not sure… I think he said 'I love you,' and he thinks I'm someone named Amanda."

# 36: BUFFALO GENERAL

Philip woke up in a white room. At first he was uncertain just where he was, then he began to look around and saw that there was a tube connected to a needle in his arm, and a wire leading to a plastic clip attached to one of his fingers. He realized that he was in a hospital.

As his mind cleared, he saw that he was in a hospital bed and that the railings were up on both sides. He vaguely remembered being struck by a car, flying into the air, landing on the asphalt. *Oh, god. How badly am I hurt? Can I —*

"Hello?" He was relieved to hear the sound of his voice. It wasn't bad enough that they had to stick a tube down his throat, or worse yet, into his neck. He remembered visiting one of his grandmothers in the hospital one time who'd had a trachaeotomy. It wasn't pleasant to see. At least he could speak.

He checked first one side and then the other. He didn't have a cast on either arm, and his legs seemed to move without any problems. Just then an aide walked in. He looked at her and said "Hello!"

"Well, hello, Mr. McReynolds. Look who's awake! I'm one of the aides; my name is Jodie. I'll let your nurse know you're back among us."

While he was waiting, he fumbled for the TV remote. It was bulky and unfamiliar, but he worked it out.

The image flashed on the screen, revealing the opening credits of the CBS Evening News. The anchor welcomed viewers and then went over the top stories of the day: a protester shot to death by a cop in a town in the Midwest. Fear of a terrorist attack from Muslim extremists. More earthquakes across places like Kansas and Oklahoma, where there never used to be earthquakes. And finally, a terrible environmental disaster in Brazil where mining waste was dumped into a river, killing thousands of fish.

Just then, the nurse walked in, taking a clipboard from a holder on the door of his room.

"Hel-*lo!* Glad to see you awake, Mr. McReynolds! You have been taking a nap for… let's see here… sixteen hours. How do you feel?" She laid the clipboard down on the side of the board, took a small penlight from her pocket, and shone it in his eye. She held up one finger. "Can you follow the movement of my finger with your eye, please?" She began to move her upraised finger around, and he followed. "Hmmm… looks good. Any residual pain, grogginess, other symptoms such as nausea, vomiting, diarrhea, constipation?"

"Well, no, but —"

"Of course, you've only just woken up. I understand. Please report if you begin experiencing any of these conditions, all right?"

"Yes, of course I —"

"Good man. Keep getting better."

She swept out of the room like the legendary white tornado.

It wasn't long until there was a knock at the door, and Philip woke up from dozing to see his door swing slightly open and who should poke her head inside but Amanda herself. It was all the aide and Amanda could do to prevent Philip from causing damage to himself as Philip scrambled to try to get to her. It was like one of those slow motion videos where the couple runs hard toward each other, except that they were caught in a slow-motion process.

Then they were holding each other, smothering each other with kisses, Amanda being careful not to injure him.

# 37: TOGETHER

Philip was in the hospital three more days before he was allowed to go home. The consensus among his doctors was that his initial injuries had been minor; no concussion, no fractures. Merely some bruises, cuts, scrapes, and contusions, all of which had been dressed a couple of days before.

"With promises from *you*" — he indicated Henry — "and *you,*" — he gestured to Amanda — "to see that he comes back if there are any complications, I see no reason why Mr. McReynolds can't return to his normal duties."

"We'll make sure he behaves, Doc," said Henry.


Philip was wheeled out to Henry's car and they drove him back to the dorm. He really wasn't seriously injured, so after getting him settled in, Henry gave Amanda strict instructions to call if there was anything they needed, and headed back to Brooklyn.

Philip and Amanda sat opposite each other, staring at each other. He realized suddenly that this was the first time the two of them had ever been completely alone together. In the past, her parents had always been around, or other moviegoers, or whatever, but now no one else was present — although Philip knew that his roommate, a guy named Kevin who he had met only once — and that in passing — could walk in on them at any time.

He was a little stiff and sore, but he insisted that he could get around all right, so they decided to go out and find something to eat at one of the many restaurants up and down Main Street.

They wound up having burgers at Louie's, and then took a quiet stroll around the campus.

"You know," said Philip quietly, "This is a nice school. Maybe you could go here instead of Rochester. It's not too late to apply."

"Maybe," Amanda smiled.

As they were walking, they passed by a small hotel and decided on the spur of the moment to find complete privacy for the first time.

When Philip actually came to bed, Amanda had already been lying comfortably for ten minutes or so, patiently waiting as Philip nervously spent time in the bathroom, cleaning up, brushing his teeth and so forth. He turned off the bathroom light and walked through the darkened room, hoping that he wouldn't do anything incredibly stupid like stub his toe.

He slipped under the covers and stretched out, savoring the feel of the crisp, clean sheets.

He rolled over and snuggled his body against hers. Being naturally warm-natured, he tended to sleep only in a pair of gym shorts; since this was unplanned, he didn't have those with him, so he was clad only in his briefs.

On this particular evening, Amanda's sleepwear of choice wasn't quite the same as what Philip had observed a few weeks before. The floral print pajamas were absent, but Philip had expected that; they hadn't planned ahead for this romantic rendezvous. But tonight, when Philip slipped his arms around her beneath the covers, he found that she was entirely nude.

He pulled her close and whispered in her ear, "I love you, Amanda."

She murmured out of the darkness, "I love you too." It had a pleasant lilt to it.

He kissed her softly and snuggled closer. His hand skimmed across the soft skin of her belly. "Mmmm," he said with a smile. "I love the way your skin feels under my hand." She sighed pleasantly in return. "Touching you makes me very, very happy." She made that same contented sound again.

"I'm enjoying it too, very much," came the whisper in the dark. He smiled and pulled her closer, letting his hand wander farther north, slowly, tentatively. His hand found her right breast and gently began to knead it, rolling the tender nipple between his fingertips. "Ooooooh," she moaned, soft and low.

"I want to touch you everywhere," Philip said. "I want to put my hands all over your body. I want to put my fingers inside you, and then my tongue, and then my…" He suddenly felt himself blushing, unable to say what he was thinking.

He had been muttering the words into her ear as he was kissing and nibbling it. He found her waiting mouth and kissed her hard, their tongues now dancing together, swirling like twin whirlpools.

Philip's hand slid down her body and began to probe between her legs. Though it was dark, in his mind he could see the pink wetness that he knew must be there, although he had never seen it. "Does that feel good?" he asked her.

"Ooooh… it feels *so* good," she replied. He felt a surge of lust and slipped two fingers inside her. It was then that he found the wetness he sought, more than he ever imagined. She let out a long, low moan, the like of which he had never heard in person.

"Do you like that, baby?" he growled into her ear. She nodded wordlessly and pulled his face toward her breasts and the hardening nipples. He bent his head and sucked her right nipple into his mouth roughly, swirling his tongue around it as he plunged two fingers back into her as far as he could.

Her juices were flowing now, and Philip was amazed that his actions could affect her like they had. Her hips were bucking now, and when he slipped one well-lubricated finger into her ass, she took it up a notch, with a nonstop stream of pleasurable moans and groans coming from her mouth.

"Oh, my *god,* that feels so good," Amanda hissed into his ear. Philip continued to fondle between her legs, rubbing her perineum between his fingers from inside her. *"Ohhhh!"* she moaned, and he felt her drip more of the sweet nectar that he had quickly come to love.

He took hold of her shoulders and began to move her, urging her up off her back into a kneeling position, and then turning her so that she faced the wood-and-metal headboard of the motel room's bed.

He instructed her to grasp the top of the headboard, which stood a foot or more above her face. She knelt there with her legs parted, her beautiful ass exposed, waiting to see what he would do next.

Philip reached over and turned on the bedside lamp, eager to be able to see her body.

Philip lowered himself to the bed so that his face was directly behind her, at ass level. He buried his face between her ass cheeks and voraciously began to lick her from behind. She squealed and her legs began to shake as she clung to the headboard. Philip ran his tongue down the crack of her gorgeous ass and scooped up some of the delicious wetness from her vaginal lips, moving back up and plunging his tongue into her, listening to her now-animalistic growling.

Philip was hard as steel now, and he knew that the time for foreplay had come and gone. With only a bit of hesitation, he grasped her waist and slid his hardness directly into her from behind, drilling for the molten center. She screamed with pleasure and he knew he had struck gold. She wailed mindlessly, now in the throes of a seemingly endless stream of orgasms.

With each explosion, he could feel her pulsing around him. After only five or six thrusts he was seriously in danger of ending this much too soon, his own orgasm threatening to explode as he teetered on the brink of ecstasy.

He pressed deep inside her and heard her gasp for air. "Does it hurt?" he said.

"Nooooooooooo," she squealed, "I'm ready, my angel — I need it, now! *Now!"*

He slid one finger down the crack of her ass and listened to her moaning. He didn't hold back. They were both ready. He shoved forward, burying himself inside her, and was rewarded with the sound of her cumming yet again. She had run out of words; her vocabulary was lost in a hurricane of pleasure, and the half a dozen or more orgasms she'd had already left her nearly catatonic, but begging for still more. Philip intended to see how many more times he could get her there before he stopped.

He knew it was almost over. He wasn't going to be able to hold back much longer, not at this rate. He felt his own pleasure boiling up, ready to explode into her like a volcano.

"Are you ready for it?" he gasped. All the energy in his body was focused in one spot, not to mention all the blood in his body having pretty much collected in his penis. He was barely able to form the words.

"Oh, yes, angel. Give it to me now! I need it!" she moaned, "Nowwwwww!"

Hearing her say something so dirty was what put him over the edge. He surrendered to the storm and let himself cum, the tsunami that was his orgasm ripping through him, blowing away what was left of his mind, erupting into her like Mount Saint Helens. She screamed with pleasure as he filled her with scalding hot, white jets, three, four, five times. He pulled out and collapsed on the bed next to her.

Amanda looked over at Philip with a dreamy look in her eyes. She smiled and kissed him, putting her arms around him and snuggling against him, her still-hard nipples grazing his chest. "Mmm," she moaned, repeating the movement several times, looking into his eyes.

He had utterly depleted her strength, it seemed, because she was lying on him now as limply as a rag doll, her face next to his. He would have worried whether he'd killed her except for the fact that he could feel her gentle breathing as she lay on him.

"You okay?" he asked. She smiled weakly and whispered, "Ohhh, yes."

Philip kissed her deeply, and they both closed their eyes and drifted off to sleep.

✕

The next morning, neither one of them wanted to get up. All they wanted to do was laze in the bed, but Amanda knew that her parents would be frantic.

At seven, Amanda called her father's cell phone and broke the news. Yes, she was with Philip. She was fine. There was no need to worry. Philip could hear her father's voice from several feet away, sounding like the buzzing of a hornet. Finally she hung up.

"Well," she said. "That went well." They laughed.

"Really?"

"Better than if I'd called my mother." They laughed some more.

✕

They went out for breakfast, then spent most of the day exploring the area. They spent a long stretch of the afternoon staring out over Lake LaSalle, simply enjoying the shimmering water.

Then Amanda turned to Philip and said, "There's something I need to tell you."

Philip turned toward her, devoting the full measure of his attention. "What is it?"

"I've decided not to go to school at Rochester."

"So you're going to apply here at SUNY?" he asked.

"No…" she said hesitantly. "You know how we talked about the fact that I am half-Japanese, and that I was adopted."

"Right…" he responded.

She took a deep breath. "I don't know how else to say this, so I'm just going to say it. I'm going to Japan, to study at Kansai Gaidai University in Osaka."

Philip looked at her as if she'd struck him. "Why did you decide to do that?"

"I want to learn more about my Japanese half, and perhaps find out where I came from. Don't worry — we're not done. I love you, my angel. But I have to find out who I am."

**Watch for the second book in this series,**

***NIGHTS IN PASAGARDA,***

**Coming soon from Five59 Publishing.**

If you obtained this book from an online bookseller, and enjoyed it, please take the time to return there and leave a review. Thanks!

Also look for these Five59 short story anthologies:

*13 Bites Volumes I, II and III* - Annual horror collection

 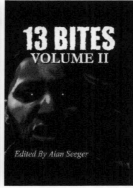 

### Other Realms
Fantasy tales

### Plan 559 From Outer Space
Science Fiction

**FIVE59.com**

FIVE FIFTY NINE QUARTERLY

Visit Five59 Publishing offers a literary web magazine published quarterly, which includes short stories, poetry and creative non-fiction.

UPCOMING ISSUES

Winter ~ February 2016

Spring ~ May 2016

Summer ~ July 2016

Fall ~ November 2016

Back issues are available at the click of a mouse.

# ABOUT THE AUTHORS

**Bruno Carlos Santos** is a resident of São Paulo, Brazil. His first novel, NOITES EM PASÁRGADA (Nights In Pasagarda), was originally published to the Brazilian Kindle store. This is an all-new English adaptation and expansion of that original story. **facebook.com/bsnovelist**

✕

Author and editor **Alan Seeger** was born in San Francisco, California, and grew up in Oklahoma. A writer for as long as he can remember, he spent much of his childhood filling spiral notebooks with his stories. In his teens, he began making music, which became his focus for the next thirty years or so. But writing was never far from his heart, and in 2013, he published his debut novel, PINBALL, the first book in his Gatespace trilogy. In December of 2013, he released the second book in the series, REPLAY. The conclusion, TILT, was published in September of 2014.

Seeger currently resides on the Rosebud Indian Reservation in South Dakota. Readers can learn more about him and his work at **alanseeger.net.**

# ABOUT FIVE59

Once upon a time, getting one's work published took a combination of luck, perseverance, and maybe even a little bit of prayer. Today, with the advent of relatively simple book publishing through various e-pub resources, anybody can be an author. *Anybody.*

No, *really.* You should see some of the stuff I've seen. The horror… the horror.

So what exactly can I do for you?

Well, first, if your book is just a hot mess of cookie cutter characters, hackneyed plot devices, and wooden dialogue, I will not be able to wave my wand and fix your book. On the other hand, if you have a book with a good story and reasonably strong characters that just needs fixes such as spelling, punctuation, grammar, and perhaps dialogue polishing, I can certainly help.

I will also look at consistency of style, content, the structure of your story, the clarity of your storytelling, your usage of terms and colloquial expressions, the consistency of your plot and proper use of syntax.

What it all boils down to is the polishing of your manuscript until it's absolutely the best it can be. I can't do these things for you without having excellent writing skills myself. This is absolutely essential to providing high quality proofing and editing services.

I've been a voracious reader and a prolific writer since I can remember; I've learned what makes a good story and how to tell it without the potholes that can jar readers out of their immersion in the story: misspelled words, incorrect punctuation and poor grammar. If you need assistance in those areas, I can help you.

I can be reached through the company website at **Five59.com.**

Alan Seeger
Five59 Publishing

Printed in Great Britain
by Amazon